Dashiell Hammett

Detective Stories and Other Writings

COYOTE CANYON PRESS
CLAREMONT, CALIFORNIA

ORIGINAL PUBLICATION HISTORY:

"The Parthian Shot." *The Smart Set*, 69, no. 2 (October 1922), 82.

"The Great Lovers." *The Smart Set*, 69, no. 3 (November 1922), 4.

"The Barber and His Wife." *Brief Stories*, 7, no. 6 (December 1922), 23–29.

"The Road Home." *The Black Mask* (December 1922).

"The Master Mind." *The Smart Set*, 70, no. 1 (January 1923), 56.

"Wages of Crime." *Brief Stories*, 8 no. 2 (February 1923), 103–106.

"From the Memoirs of a Private Detective." *The Smart Set*, 70, no. 3 (March 1923), 87–90.

"The Man Who Stood in the Way." *The Black Mask*, 6, no. 6 (15 June 1923), 106–111.

"The Joke on Eloise Morey." *Brief Stories*, 8, no. 4 (June 1923), 295–298.

"Holiday." *The New Pearsons*, 49. no. 7 (July 1923), 30–32.

"Arson Plus." *The Black Mask*, 6, no. 13 (1 October 1923), 25–36.

"In the Morgue." *Saucy Stories*, 15, no. 2 (15 October 1923), 115–116.

"Crooked Souls." *The Black Mask*, 6, no. 14 (15 October 1923), 35–44.

"Slippery Fingers." *The Black Mask*, 6, no. 14 (15 October 1923), 96–103.

"The Green Elephant." *The Smart Set*, 73, no. 2 (October 1923), 103–108.

"The Black Hat That Wasn't There." *The Black Mask*, 6, no. 15 (1 November 1923), 110–118.

"The Second-Story Angel." *The Black Mask*, 6, no. 16 (15 November 1923), 110–118.

"When Luck's Running Good." *Action Stories*, 3, no. 3 (November 1923), 61–81.

"Bodies Piled Up." *The Black Mask*, 6, no. 17 (1 December 1923), 33–42.

CONTENTS

THE PARTHIAN SHOT

WHEN THE boy was six months old Paulette Key acknowledged that her hopes and efforts had been futile, that the baby was indubitably and irremediably a replica of its father. She could have endured the physical resemblance, but the duplication of Harold Key's stupid obstinacy—unmistakable in the fixity of the child's inarticulate demands for its food, its toys—was too much for Paulette. She knew she could not go on living with *two* such natures! A year and a half of Harold's domination had not subdued her entirely. She took the little boy to church, had him christened Don, sent him home by his nurse, and boarded a train for the west.

THE GREAT LOVERS

NOW THAT the meek and the humble have inherited the earth
and it were arrogance to look down upon any man—the apologetic
being the mode in lives—I should like to go monthly to some hidden gallery and, behind drawn curtains, burn perfumed candles
before the images of:

Joachim Murat, King of Naples, who mourned, "Ah, the poor
people! They are ignorant of the misfortune they are about to suffer. They do not know that I am going away."

The Earl of Chatham, who said, "My lord, I am sure I can save
the country and no one else can."

Louis XIV of France, who perhaps said, *"L'etat c'est moi,"* and who,
upon receiving news of the battle of Ramillies, cried, "God has
then forgotten all that I have done for Him!"

William Rufus, who held that if he had duties toward God, God
also had duties toward him.

Prince Metternich, who wrote in his diary, "Fain's memoirs of
the year 1813 are worth reading—they contain my history as well
as Napoleon's"; and who said of his daughter, "She is very like my
mother; therefore possesses some of my charm."

Joseph II of Austria, who said, "If I wish to walk with my equals,
then I must go to the Capuchin

Charles IV of Spain, who, playing in a quartet, ignored a three-
bar pause which occurred in his part; and upon being told of his
mistake by Olivieri laid down his bow in amazement, protesting,

"The king never wails for anyone!"

The Prince of Kaunitz Rietberg, whose highest praise was, "Even I could not have done it better"; and who said, "Heaven takes a hundred years to form a great genius for the generation of an empire, after which it rests a hundred years. This makes me tremble for the Austrian monarchy after my death."

Virginicchia Oldoni, Countess of Castiglione, who kissed the baby, saying, "When he is grown up you will tell him that the first kiss he ever received was given him by the most beautiful woman of the century."

The Lord Brougham, who paid for his dinner with a cheque, explaining to his companions, "I have plenty of money, but, don't you see, the host may prefer my signature to the money."

Paul of Russia, who had his horse given fifty strokes, exclaiming, "There, that is for having stumbled with the emperor!"

And Thomas Hart Benton, who, when his publishers consulted him concerning the number of copies of his book, *Thirty Years' View*, to be printed, replied, "Sir, you can ascertain from the last census how many persons there are in the United States who can read, sir"; and who refused to speak against Calhoun when he was ill, saying, "When God Almighty lays His hands on a man, Benton takes his off!" . . .

THE BARBER AND HIS WIFE

EACH MORNING at seven thirty the alarm clock on the table beside their bed awakened the Stemlers to perform their daily comedy—a comedy that varied from week to week in degree only.

Louis Stemler, disregarding the still-ringing clock, leaped out of bed and went to the open window, where he stood inhaling and exhaling with a great show of enjoyment—throwing out his chest and stretching his arms voluptuously. He enjoyed this most in the winter, and would prolong his stay before the open window until his body was icy under his pajamas. In the coast city where the Stemlers lived the morning breezes were chill enough, whatever the season, to make his display of ruggedness sufficiently irritating to Pearl.

Meanwhile, Pearl had turned off the alarm and closed her eyes again in semblance of sleep. Louis was reasonably confident that his wife was still awake; but he could not be certain. So when he ran into the bathroom to turn on the water in the tub, he was none too quiet.

He then re-entered the bedroom to go through an elaborate and complicated set of exercises, after which he returned to the bathroom, got into the tub and splashed merrily—long enough to assure any listener that to him a cold bath was a thing of pleasure. Rubbing himself with a coarse towel, he began whistling; and always it was a tune reminiscent of the First World War. Just now *Keep the Home Fires Burning* was his choice. This was his favorite, rivaled only by *'Till We Meet Again,* though occasionally he rendered *Katy, What Are You Going to Do to Help the Boys,* or *How're You Going to Keep Them Down on the Farm.* He whistled low and flatly, keeping time with the brisk movements of the towel. At this point Pearl would usually give way to her irritation to the extent of turning over in bed, and the rustling of the sheets would come pleasantly from the bedroom to her husband's ears. This morning as she turned she sighed faintly, and Louis, his eager ears catching the sound, felt a glow of satisfaction.

Dry and ruddy, he came back to the bedroom and began dressing, whistling under his breath and paying as little apparent attention to Pearl as she to him, though each was on the alert for any chance opening through which the other might be vexed. Long practice in this sort of warfare had schooled them to such a degree, however, that an opening seldom presented itself. Pearl was at a decided disadvantage in these morning encounters, inasmuch as she was on the defensive, and her only weapon was a pretense of sleep in the face of her husband's posturing. Louis, even aside from his wife's vexation, enjoyed every bit of his part in the silent wrangle; the possibility that perhaps after all she was really asleep and not witnessing his display of manliness was the only damper on his enjoyment.

When Louis had one foot in his trousers, Pearl got out of bed and into her kimono and slippers, dabbed a little warm water on her face, and went into the kitchen to prepare breakfast. In the ensuing race she forgot her slight headache. It was a point of honor with her never to rise until her husband had his trousers in his hand, and then to have his breakfast on the table in the kitchen—where they ate it—by the time he was dressed. Thanks to the care with which he knotted his necktie, she usually succeeded. Louis's aim, of course, was to arrive in the kitchen fully dressed and with the morning paper in his hand before the meal was ready, and to be extremely affable over the delay. This morning, as a concession to a new shirt—a white silk one with broad cerise stripes—he went in to breakfast without his coat and vest, surprising Pearl in the act of pouring the coffee.

"Breakfast ready, pet?" he asked.

"It will be by the time you're dressed," his wife called attention to his departure from the accepted code.

And so this morning honors were about even . . .

Louis read the sports pages while he ate, with occasional glances at his cerise-striped sleeves. He was stimulated by the clash between the stripe and his crimson sleeve-garters. He had a passion for red, and it testified to the strength of the taboos of his kind that he did not wear red neckties.

"How do you feel this morning, pet?" he asked after he had read what a reporter had to say about the champion's next fight, and before he started on the account of the previous day's ball games.

"All right."

Pearl knew that to mention the headache would be to invite a display of superiority masked as sympathy, and perhaps an admonition to eat more beef, and certainly one to take more exercise; for Louis, never having experienced any of the ills to which the flesh is heir, was, naturally enough, of the opinion that even where such disorders were really as painful as their possessors' manners would indicate, they could have been avoided by proper care.

Breakfast consumed, Louis lighted a cigar and addressed himself to another cup of coffee. With the lighting of the cigar Pearl brightened a little. Louis, out of consideration for his lungs, smoked without inhaling; and to Pearl this taking of smoke into the mouth and blowing it forth seemed silly and childish. Without putting it into words she had made this opinion known to her husband, and whenever he smoked at home she watched him with a quiet interest which, of all her contrivances, was the most annoying to him. But that it would have been so signal an admission of defeat, he would have given up smoking at home.

The sports pages read—with the exceptions of the columns devoted to golf and tennis—Louis left the table, put on his vest, coat, and hat, kissed his wife, and, with his consciously buoyant step, set out for his shop. He always walked downtown in the morning, covering the twenty blocks in twenty minutes—a feat to which he would allude whenever the opportunity arose ...

Louis entered his shop with a feeling of pride in no wise lessened by six years of familiarity. To him the shop was as wonderful, as beautiful, as it had been when first opened. The row of green and white automatic chairs, with white-coated barbers bending over the shrouded occupants; the curtained alcoves in the rear with white-gowned manicurists in attendance; the table laden with magazines and newspapers; the clothes-trees; the row of white enameled chairs, at this hour holding no waiting customers; the two Negro bootblacks in their white jackets; the clusters of colored bottles; the smell of tonics and soaps and steam; and around all, the sheen of spotless tiling, porcelain and paint and polished mirrors. Louis stood just within the door and basked in all this while he acknowledged his employees' greetings. All had been with him for more than a year now, and they called him "Lou" in just the correct tone of respectful familiarity—a tribute both to his position in their world and to his geniality.

He walked the length of the shop, trading jests with his barbers—pausing for a moment to speak to George Fielding, real estate, who was having his pink face steamed preparatory to his biweekly massage—and then gave his coat and hat to Percy, one of the bootblacks, and dropped into Fred's chair for his shave. Around him the odor of lotions and the hum of mechanical devices rose soothingly. Health and this ... where did those pessimists get their stuff?

The telephone in the front of the shop rang, and Emil, the head-barber, called out, "Your brother wants to talk to you, Lou."

"Tell him I'm shaving. What does he want?"

Emil spoke into the instrument; then, "He wants to know if you

9

can come over to his office some time this morning."

"Tell him all right!'"

"Another big deal?" Fielding asked.

"You'd be surprised," Louis replied, in accordance with the traditional wit of barbers.

Fred gave a final pat to Louis's face with a talcumed towel, Percy a final pat to his glowing shoes, and the proprietor stepped from the chair to hide the cerise stripes within his coat again.

"I'm going over to see Ben," he told Emil. "I'll be back in an hour or so."

Ben Stemler, the eldest of four brothers, of which Louis was the third, was a round, pallid man, always out of breath—as if he had just climbed a long flight of steps. He was district sales-manager for a New York manufacturer, and attributed his moderate success, after years of struggling, to his doggedness in refusing to accept defeat. Chronic nephritis, with which he had been afflicted of late years, was more truly responsible for his increased prosperity, however. It had puffed out his face around his protuberant, fishy eyes, subduing their prominence, throwing kindly shadows over their fishiness, and so giving to him a more trustworthy appearance.

Ben was dictating pantingly to his stenographer when Louis entered the office. "Your favor of the . . . would say . . . regret our inability to comply . . . your earliest convenience." He nodded to his brother and went on gasping. "Letter to Schneider . . . are at a loss to understand . . . our Mr. Rose . . ."

The dictation brought to a wheezing end, he sent the stenographer out, and turned to Louis.

"How's everything?" Louis asked.

"Could be worse, Lou, but I don't feel so good."

"Trouble is you don't get enough exercise. Get out and walk; let me take you down to the gym; take cold baths."

"I know, I know," Ben said wearily. "Maybe you're right. But I got something to tell you—something you ought to know—but I don't know how to go about telling you. I—that is—"

"Spit it out!" Louis was smiling. Ben probably had got into trouble of some sort.

"It's about Pearl!" Ben was gasping now, as if he had come from an unusually steep flight of steps.

"Well?" Louis had stiffened in his chair, but the smile was still on his face. He wasn't a man to be knocked over by the first blow. He had never thought of Pearl's being unfaithful before, but as soon as Ben mentioned her name he knew that was it. He knew it without another word from Ben; it seemed so much the inevitable thing that he wondered at his never having suspected it.

"Well?" he asked again.

Unable to hit upon a way of breaking the news gently, Ben panted it out hurriedly, anxious to have the job off his hands. "I saw her night before last. At the movies. With a man. Norman Becker! Sells for Litz & Aulitz. They left together—in his car. Bertha was with me—she saw 'em too!"

He closed with a gasp of relief and relapsed into wheezes.

"Night before last," Louis mused. "I was down to the fights—Kid Breen knocked out O'Toole in the second round—and I didn't get home until after one."

From Ben's office to Louis's home was a distance of twenty-four blocks. Mechanically timing himself, he found it had taken him thirty-one minutes—much of the way was uphill—pretty good time at that. Louis had elected to walk home, he told himself, because he had plenty of time, not because he needed time to think the situation over, or anything of that sort. There was nothing to think over. This was a crystal-clear, tangible condition. He had a wife. Another man had encroached, or perhaps only attempted to, on his proprietorship. To a red-blooded he-man the solution was obvious. For these situations men had fists and muscles and courage. For these emergencies men ate beef, breathed at open windows, held memberships in athletic clubs, and kept tobacco smoke out of their lungs. The extent of the encroachment determined, the rest would be simple.

Pearl looked up in surprise from the laundering of some silk things.

"Where were you night before last?" His voice was calm and steady.

"At the movies." Pearl's voice was too casual. The casual was not the note she should have selected—but she knew what was coming anyway.

"Who with?"

Recognizing the futility of any attempt at deception, Pearl fell back upon the desire to score upon the other at any cost—the motive underlying all their relations since the early glamor of mating had worn off.

"With a man! I went there to meet him. I've met him places before. He wants me to go away with him. He reads things besides the sporting-page. He doesn't go to prizefights. He likes the movies. He doesn't like burlesque shows. He inhales cigarette smoke. He doesn't think muscle's everything a man ought to have." Her voice rose high and shrill.

Louis cut into her tirade with a question. He was surprised by her outburst, but he was not a man to be unduly excited by his wife's display of nerves.

"No, not yet, but if I want to I will," Pearl answered the question with scarcely a break in her high-pitched chant. "And if I want to, I'll go away with him. He doesn't want beef for every meal. He doesn't take cold baths. He can appreciate things that aren't just brutal. He doesn't worship his body. He—"

As Louis closed the door behind him he heard his wife's shrill voice still singing her wooer's qualities.

"Is Mr. Becker in?" Louis asked the undersized boy behind a railing in the sales-office of Litz & Aulitz.

"That's him at the desk back in the corner."

Louis opened the gate and walked down the long office between two rows of mathematically arranged desks—two flat desks, a typist, two flat desks, a typist. A rattle of typewriters, a rustling of papers, a drone of voices dictating: "Your favor of . . . our Mr. Hassis . . . would say . . ." Walking with his consciously buoyant step, Louis studied the man in the corner. Built well enough, but probably flabby and unable to stand up against body blows.

He stopped before Becker's desk and the younger man looked up at Louis through pale, harassed eyes.

"Is this Mr. Becker?"

"Yes, sir. Won't you have a seat?"

"No," Louis said evenly, "what I'm going to say ought to be said standing up." He appreciated the bewilderment in the salesman's eyes. "I'm Louis Stemler!"

"Oh! yes," said Becker. Obviously he could think of nothing else to say. He reached for an order blank, but with it in his hand he was still at sea.

I'm going to teach you," Louis said, "not to fool around with other men's wives."

Becker's look of habitual harassment deepened. Something foolish was going to happen. One could see he had a great dread of being made ridiculous.

"Will you get up?" Louis was unbuttoning his coat.

In the absence of an excuse for remaining seated, Becker got vaguely to his feet. Louis stepped around the corner of the desk and faced the salesman.

I'm giving you an even break," Louis said, shoulders stiffened, left foot advanced, eyes steady on the embarrassed ones before him.

Becker nodded politely.

The barber shifted his weight from right to left leg and struck the younger man on the mouth, knocking him back against the wall. The confusion in Becker's face changed to anger. So this was what it was to be! He rushed at Louis, to be met by blows that shook him, forced him back, battered him down. Blindly he tried to hold the barber's arms, but the arms writhed free and the fists clashed into his face and body again and again. Becker hadn't walked twenty blocks in twenty minutes, hadn't breathed deeply at open windows, hadn't twisted and lowered and raised and bent his body morning after morning, hadn't spent hours in gymnasiums building up sinew. Such an emergency found him wanting.

Men crowded around the combatants, separating them, holding them apart, supporting Becker, whose legs were sagging.

Louis was breathing easily. He regarded the salesman's bloody face with calm eyes, and said: "After this I guess you won't bother my wife any. If I ever hear of you even saying 'how do' to her again I'll come back and finish the job. Get me?"

Becker nodded dumbly.

Louis adjusted his necktie and left the office.

The matter was cleanly and effectually disposed of. No losing his wife, no running into divorce courts, no shooting or similar cheap melodrama, and above all, no getting into the newspapers as a deceived husband—just a sensible, manly solution of the problem.

He would eat downtown tonight and go to a burlesque show afterward, and Pearl's attack of nerves would have subsided by the time he got home. He would never mention the events of this day, unless some extraordinary emergency made it advisable, but his wife would know that it was always in his mind, and that he had demonstrated his ability to protect what was his.

He telephoned Pearl. Her voice came quietly over the wire. The hysteria had run its course, then. She asked no questions and made no comment upon his intention of remaining downtown for the evening meal.

It was long after midnight when he arrived home. After the show he had met "Dutch" Spreel, the manager of "Oakland Kid McCoy, the most promising lightweight since the days of Young Terry Sullivan," and had spent several hours in a lunchroom listening to Spreel's condemnation of the guile whereby the Kid had been robbed of victory in his last battle—a victory to which the honest world unanimously conceded his right.

Louis let himself into the apartment quietly and switched on the light in the vestibule. Through the open bedroom door he saw that the bed was unoccupied and its surface unruffled. Where was Pearl, then? Surely she wasn't sitting up in the dark. He went through the rooms, switching on the lights.

On the dining-room table he found a note.

I never want to see you again, you brute. It was just like you—as if beating Norman would do any good. I have gone away with him.

Louis leaned against the table while his calm certitude ran out of him. So this was the world! He had given Becker his chance; hadn't taken the advantage of him to which he had been entitled; had beaten him severely—and this was the way it turned out. Why, a man might just as well be a weakling!

THE ROAD HOME

"YOU'RE A fool to pass it up! You'll get just as much credit and reward for taking back proof of my death as you will for taking me back. And I got papers and stuff buried back near the Yunnan border that you can have to back up your story, and you needn't be afraid that I'll ever show up to spoil your play."

The gaunt man in faded khaki frowned with patient annoyance and looked away from the bloodshot brown eyes in front of him, over the teak side of the *jahaz* to where the wrinkled snout of a *muggar* broke the surface of the river. When the small crocodile submerged again, Hagedom's gray eyes came back to the pleading ones before him, and he spoke wearily, as one who has been answering the same arguments again and again.

"I can't do it, Barnes. I left New York two years ago to get you, and for two years I've been in this damned country—here and in Yunnan—hunting you. I promised my people I'd stay until I found you, and I kept my word. Lord! man," with a touch of exasperation, "after all I've gone through you don't expect me to throw them down now—now that the job's as good as done!"

The dark man in the garb of a native smiled an oily, ingratiating smile and brushed away his captor's words with a wave of his hand.

"I ain't offering you a dinky coupla thousand dollars; I'm offering you your pick out of one of the richest gem beds in Asia—a bed that was hidden by the *Mran-ma* when the British jumped the country. Come back up there with me and I'll show you rubies

16

and sapphires and topazes that'll knock your eye out. All I'm asking you is to go back up there with me and take a look at 'em. If
you don't like 'em you'll still have me to take back to New York."

Hagedorn shook his head slowly.

"You're going back to New York with me. Maybe man-hunting
isn't the nicest trade in the world but it's all the trade I've got, and
this jewel bed of yours sounds phoney to me. I can't blame you for
not wanting to go back—but just the same I'm taking you."

Barnes glared at the detective disgustedly.

"You're a fine chump! And it's costing me and you thousands
of dollars! Hell!"

He spat over the side insultingly—native-like—and settled
himself back on his corner of the split-bamboo mat.

Hagedorn was looking past the lateen sail, down the river—
the beginning of the route to New York—along which a miasmal
breeze was carrying the fifty-foot boat with surprising speed. Four
more days and they would be aboard a steamer for Rangoon; then
another steamer to Calcutta, and in the end, one to New York—
home, after two years!

Two years through unknown country, pursuing what until the
very day of the capture had never been more than a vague shadow. Through Yunnan and Burma, combing wilderness with mi-
croscopic thoroughness—a game of hide-and-seek up the rivers,
over the hills and through the jungles—sometimes a year, sometimes two months and then six behind his quarry. And now suc-
cessfully home! Betty would be fifteen—quite a lady.

Barnes edged forward and resumed his pleading, with a whine
creeping into his voice.

"Say, Hagedorn, why don't you listen to reason? There ain't no
sense in us losing all that money just for something that happened
over two years ago. I didn't mean to kill that guy, anyway.

You know how it is; I was a kid and wild and foolish—but I wasn't
mean—and I got in with a bunch. Why, I thought of that holdup as a lark when we planned it! And then that messenger yelled

and I guess I was excited, and my gun went off the first thing I knew. I didn't go to kill him; and it won't do him no good to take me back and hang me for it. The express company didn't lose no money. What do they want to hound me like this for? I been trying to live it down."

The gaunt detective answered quietly enough but what kindness there had been in his dry voice before was gone now.

"I know—the old story! And the bruises on the Burmese woman you were living with sure show that there's nothing mean about you. Cut it, Barnes, and make up your mind to face it—you and I are going back to New York."

"The hell we are!"

Barnes got slowly to his feet and backed away a step.

"I'd just as leave—"

Hagedorn's automatic came out a split second too late; his prisoner was over the side and swimming toward the bank. The detective caught up his rifle from the deck behind him and sprang to the rail. Barnes' head showed for a moment and then went down again, to appear again twenty feet nearer shore. Upstream the man in the boat saw the blunt, wrinkled noses of three *muggars*, moving toward the shore at a tangent that would intercept the fugitive. He leaned against the teak rail and summed up the situation.

"Looks like I'm not going to take him back alive after all—but my job's done. I can shoot him when he shows again, or I can let him alone and the *muggars* will get him."

Then the sudden but logical instinct to side with the member of his own species against enemies from another wiped out all other considerations, and sent his rifle to his shoulder to throw a shower of bullets into the *muggars*.

Barnes clambered up the bank of the river, waved his hand over his head without looking back, and plunged into the jungle.

Hagedorn turned to the bearded owner of the *jahaz*, who had come to his side, and addressed him in his broke Burmese.

"Put me ashore—*yu nga apau mye*—and wait—*thaing*—until I

bring him back—*thu yughe.*"

The captain wagged his black beard protestingly.

"*Mahok!* In the jungle here, *sahib*, a man is as a leaf. Twenty men might find him in a week, or a month, it may take five years. I cannot wait that long."

The gaunt white man gnawed at his lower lip and looked down the river—the road to New York.

"Two years," he said aloud to himself, "it took to find him when he didn't know I was hunting for him. Now—Oh, hell! It may take five years. I wonder about them jewels of his."

He turned to the boatman.

"I go after him. You wait three hours," pointing overhead, "until noon—*ne apomha.* If I am not back then do not wait—*malotu thaing, thwa. Thi?*"

The captain nodded.

"*Hokhe!*"

For five hours the captain kept the *jahaz* at anchor, and then, when the shadows of the trees on the west bank were creeping out into the river, he ordered the latten sail hoisted, and the teak craft vanished around a bend in the river.

THE MASTER MIND

WHEREVER CRIME or criminals were discussed by enlightened folk, the name of Waldron Honeywell could be heard. It was a symbol—to the citizens of Punta Arenas no less than to those of Tammerfors—for the ultimate in the prevention and detection of crime. A native of the United States, Honeywell's work had overflowed the national boundaries. Thirty years of warfare upon crime had taken him into every quarter of the globe, and his fame into every nook where the printed word penetrated.

Bringing to his work a singularly perspicacious intellect, and combining an exhaustive knowledge of both the scientific and more practical phases of his profession, he had reduced it to as nearly exact a science as possible; and his supremacy in his field had never been questioned.

He had punctured Lombroso's theories at a time when the scientific world regarded the Italian as a Messiah. The treatise with which he exploded the belief—fostered by no less an authority than the great W. J. Burns—that Sir Arthur Conan Doyle would have made a successful detective, and showed that the mysteries confronting Sherlock Holmes would have been susceptible to the routine methods of the ordinary policeman, was familiar to the readers of eight languages. The mastery with which he unearthed and frustrated the Versailles bomb plot before it was well on its feet; the dispatch with which he recovered the aircraft program memoranda; his success in finding the assassin of the emperor of

Abyssinia, the details of which were suppressed for some obscure political reason; the effectual manner in which he coped with the epidemic of postal robberies—these were matters of history, but in no way more remarkable than a thousand-odd other exploits in which he had figured.

Honors and decorations were showered upon him, governments sought his advice, scientists deferred to him, criminals shuddered at the sound of his name (one, who had avoided arrest for seventeen years, surrendered to the nearest policeman upon learning that Honeywell had been engaged to hunt him down), and his monetary rewards were enormous.

Early in 1922 Waldron Honeywell died, and left an estate consisting of $182.65 in cash, 37,500 shares of International Solar Power Corporation common, 42,555 shares of Cousin Tilly Gold, Platinum & Diamond Mining Company common, 6,430 shares of Universal Petroleum Corporation of Uruguay, S. A. preferred, and 75,000 shares of New Era Fuelless Motor Company common.

WAGES OF CRIME

COME ALONG without any fuss and there won't be trouble," said the tall man with the protruding lower lip.

"And remember, anything you say will—" the fat man under the stiff straw hat warned, the rest of the prescribed caution dying somewhere within the folds of his burly neck.

A frown of perplexed interrogation reduced the none too ample area between Tom Doody's eyebrows and the roots of his hair. He cleared his throat uneasily and asked, "But what's it for?"

The protruding lower lip overlapped the upper in a smile that tempered derision with indulgence. "You ought to be able to guess—but it ain't a secret. You're arrested for stealing sixty-five thousand dollars from the National Marine Bank. We found the dough where you hid it, and now we got you."

"That's what," the fat man corroborated.

Tom Doody leaned across the plain table in the visitors' room and bent his beady eyes on the tired, middle-aged eyes of the woman from the *Morning Bulletin*.

"Miss Envers, I have served three and a half years here and I've got nearly ten more to do, taking in account what I expect to get off for good behavior. A long time, I guess you think; but I'm telling you that I don't regret a minute of it." He paused to let this startling assertion sink in, and then leaned forward again over hands that lay flat, palms down, fingers spread, on the top of the table.

"I came in here, Miss Envers, a safe-burglar that had been caught for the first and only time in fifteen years of crime. I am going out of here completely reformed, and with only one aim in my life; and that's to do all I can to keep other people from following in my footsteps. I'm studying, and the chaplain is helping me, so that when I get out I can talk and write so as to get my message across. I used to be pretty good at reciting and making speeches when I was a kid in school and I guess it'll come back to me all right. I'm going from one end of the country to the other, if I have to ride freights, telling of my experiences as a criminal, and the light that busted—burst on me here in prison. I know what it is, and lots of people that maybe wouldn't listen to a preacher or anybody else will pay attention to me. They'll know that I know what I am talking about, that I've been through it, that I'm the man who robbed the National Marine Bank and lots of others."

"You were very nearly acquitted, weren't you?" Evelyn Envers asked.

"Yes, nearly," the convict said, "and as truly as I'm sitting here, Miss Envers, I thank God that I was convicted!"

He stopped and tried to read surprise in the faded gray eyes across the table. Then he went on. "But for that—the chance for self-knowledge and thought that this place has gave—has given me—I might have gone on and on, might never have come to an understanding of what it means to be a Christian and know the difference between right and wrong. Here in prison I found for the first time in my life, liberty—yes liberty!—freedom from the bonds of vice and crime and self-destruction!" With this paradox he rested.

"Have you made any other plans for your career after leaving here?" the woman asked.

"No. That's too far ahead. But I am going to spend the rest of my life spreading the truth about crime as I know it, if I have to sleep in gutters and live on stale bread!"

"He's a fraud, of course," Evelyn Envers told her typewriter as she slid a sheet of paper into it, "but he'll make as good a story as anything else."

So she wrote a column about Tom Doody and his high resolves, and because the thought behind his reformation was so evident to her she took special pains with the story, gilding the shabbier of his mouthings and garnishing the man himself with no inconsiderable appeal.

For several days after the story's appearance letters came to the *Morning Bulletin* Readers' Forum, commenting on Tom Doody and tendering suggestions of various sorts.

The Rev. Randall Gordon Rand made Tom Doody the subject of one of his informal Sunday talks.

And then John J. Kelleher, 1322 Britton Street, was crushed to death by a furniture van after pushing little Fern Bier, five-year-old daughter of Louis Bier, 1304 Britton Street, to safety; and it developed that Kelleher had been convicted of burglary several years before, and was out on parole at the time of the accident.

Evelyn Envers wrote a column about Kelleher and his dark-eyed little wife, and with doubtful relevance brought Tom Doody into the last paragraph. The *Chronicle* and the *Intelligencer* printed editorials in which Kelleher's death was adduced as demonstrative of the parole system's merit.

On the afternoon before the next regular meeting of the State Parole Board the football team of the state university—three members of the board were ardent alumni—turned a defeat into victory in the last quarter.

Tom Doody was paroled.

From his room on the third floor of the Chapham Hotel, Tom Doody could see one of the posters. Red and black letters across a fifteen-by-thirty field of glaring white gave notice that Tom Doody, a reformed safe-burglar of considerable renown, would talk at the Lyric Theater each night for one week on the wages of sin.

Tom Doody tilted his chair forward, rested his elbows on the sill, and studied the poster with fond eyes. That billboard was all right—though he had thought perhaps his picture would be on it. But Fincher had displayed no enthusiasm when a suggestion to that effect had been made, and whatever Fincher said went. Fincher was all right. There was the contract Fincher had given him—a good hundred dollars more a week than he had really expected. And then there was that young fellow Fincher had hired to put Tom Doody's lecture in shape. There was no doubt that the lecture was all right now.

The lecture began with his childhood in the bosom of a loving family, carried him through the usual dance-hall and pool-room introductions to gay society, and then rose in a crescendo of vague but nevertheless increasingly vicious crime to a smashing climax with the burglary of the National Marine Bank's $65,000, the resultant arrest and conviction, and the new life that had dawned as he bent one day over his machine in the prison jute-mill. Then a tapering off with a picture of the criminal's inherent misery and the glory of standing four-square with the world. But the red meat of it was the thousand and one nights of crime—that was what the audience would come to hear.

The young fellow who had been hired to mold and polish the Doody epic had wanted concrete facts—names and dates and amounts—about the earlier crimes; but Tom Doody had drawn the line there, protesting that such a course would lay him open to arrest for felonies with which the police had heretofore been unable to connect him, and Fincher had agreed with him.

The truth of it was that there were no crimes prior to the National Marine Bank burglary—that unexpected conviction was the only picturesque spot in Tom Doody's life. But he knew too much to tell Fincher that. At the time of his arrest the newspapers and the police—who, for quite perceptible reasons, pretend to see in every apprehended criminal an enormously adept and industrious fellow—had brought to light hundreds of burglaries, and even a murder or two, in which this Tom Doody might have been implicated. He felt that these fanciful accusations had helped expedite his conviction, but now the fanfare was to be of value to him—as witness the figure on his contract. As a burglar with but a single crime to his credit he would have been a poor attraction on the platform, but with the sable and crimson laurels the police and the press had hung upon him, that was another matter.

For at least a year these black and red and white posters would accompany him wherever he went. His contract covered that period, and perhaps he could renew it for many years. Why not? The lecture was all right, and he knew he could deliver it creditably. He had rehearsed assiduously and Fincher had seemed pleased with his address. Of course he'd probably be a little nervous to-morrow night, when he faced an audience for the first time, but that would pass and he would soon feel at home in this new game. There was money in it—the ticket sales had been large, so Fincher said. Perhaps after a while—

The door opened violently and Fincher came into the room— an apoplectic Fincher, altogether unlike the usual smiling, mellow manager of Fincher's International Lecture Bureau.

"What's up?" Tom Doody asked, consciously keeping his eyes from darting furtively toward the door.

"What's up?" Fincher repeated the words, but his voice was a bellow. "What's up?" He brandished a rolled newspaper shillalah-wise* in Tom Doody's face. "I'll show you what's up!" He seemed to be lashing himself into more vehement fury with reiterations of the ex-convict's query, as lions were once said to do with their tails.

He straightened out the newspaper, smoothed a few square inches of its surface, and thrust it at Tom Doody's nose, with one lusty forefinger laid like an indicator on the center of the sheet. Tom Doody leaned back until his eyes were far enough away to focus upon the print around his manager's finger.

---

* With the force of the Shillalah Creek.

. . . by the police, Tom Doody, who was paroled several days ago after serving nearly four years for the theft of $65,000 from the National Marine Bank, has been completely exonerated of that crime by the deathbed confession of Walter Beadle, who . . .

"That's what's up!" Fincher shouted, when Tom Doody had shifted his abject eyes from the paper to the floor. "Now I want that five hundred dollars I advanced to you!"

Tom Doody went through his pockets with alacrity that poorly masked his despair, and brought out some bills and a handful of silver. Fincher grabbed the money from the ex-convict's hands and counted it rapidly.

"Two hundred and thirty-one dollars and forty cents," he announced. "Where's the rest?"

Tom Doody tried to say something but only muttered.

"Mumbling won't do any good," Fincher snarled. "I want my five hundred dollars. Where is it?"

"That's all I've got," Tom Doody whined. "I spent the rest, but I'll pay every cent of it back if you'll only give me time."

"I'll give you time, you dirty crook, I'll give you time!" Fincher stamped to the telephone. "I'll give you till the police get here, and if you don't come across I'm going to swear out a warrant for obtaining money under false pretenses!"

FROM THE MEMOIRS OF A PRIVATE DETECTIVE

1

WISHING TO get some information from members of the W. C. T. U. in an Oregon city, I introduced myself as the secretary of the Butte Civic Purity League. One of them read me a long discourse on the erotic effects of cigarettes upon young girls. Subsequent experiments proved this trip worthless.

2

A man whom I was shadowing went out into the country for a walk one Sunday afternoon and lost his bearings completely. I had to direct him back to the city.

3

House burglary is probably the poorest paid trade in the world; I have never known anyone to make a living at it. But for that matter few criminals of any class are self-supporting unless they toil at something legitimate between times. Most of them, however, live on their women.

4

I know an operative who while looking for pickpockets at the Havre de Grace race track had his wallet stolen. He later became an official in an Eastern detective agency.

5

Three times I have been mistaken for a Prohibition agent, but never had any trouble clearing myself.

6

Taking a prisoner from a ranch near Gilt Edge, Mont., to Lewistown one night, my machine broke down and we had to sit there until daylight. The prisoner, who stoutly affirmed his innocence, was clothed only in overalls and shirt. After shivering all night on the front seat his morale was low, and I had no difficulty in getting a complete confession from him while walking to the nearest ranch early the following morning.

7

Of all the men embezzling from their employers with whom I have had contact, I can't remember a dozen who smoked, drank, or had any of the vices in which bonding companies are so interested.

8

I was once falsely accused of perjury and had to perjure myself to escape arrest.

9

A detective agency official in San Francisco once substituted "truthful" for "voracious" in one of my reports on the grounds that the client might not understand the latter. A few days later in another report "simulate" became "quicken" for the same reason.

10

Of all the nationalities haled into the criminal courts, the Greek is the most difficult to convict. He simply denies everything, no matter how conclusive the proof may be; and nothing so impresses a jury as a bare statement of fact, regardless of the fact's inherent improbability or obvious absurdity in the face of overwhelming contrary evidence.

11

I know a man who will forge the impressions of any set of fingers in the world for $50.

12

I have never known a man capable of turning out first-rate work in a trade, a profession or an art, who was a professional criminal.

13

I know a detective who once attempted to disguise himself thoroughly. The first policeman he met took him into custody.

14

I know a deputy sheriff in Montana who, approaching the cabin of a homesteader for whose arrest he had a warrant, was confronted by the homesteader with a rifle in his hands. The deputy sheriff drew his revolver and tried to shoot over the homesteader's head to frighten him. The range was long and a strong wind was blowing. The bullet knocked the rifle from the homesteader's hands. As time went by the deputy sheriff came to accept as the truth the reputation for expertness that this incident gave him, and he not only let his friends enter him in a shooting contest, but wagered everything he owned upon his skill. When the contest was held he missed the target completely with all six shots.

15

Once in Seattle the wife of a fugitive swindler offered to sell me a photograph of her husband for $15. I knew where I could get one free, so I didn't buy it.

16

I was once engaged to discharge a woman's housekeeper.

17

The slang in use among criminals is for the most part a conscious, artificial growth, designed more to confuse outsiders than for any other purpose, but sometimes it is singularly expressive; for instance, *two-time loser*—one who has been convicted twice; and the older *gone to read and write*—found it advisable to go away for a while.

18

Pocket-picking is the easiest to master of all the criminal trades. Anyone who is not crippled can become an adept in a day.

19

In 1917, in Washington, D. C, I met a young woman who did not remark that my work must be very interesting.

20

Even where the criminal makes no attempt to efface the prints of his fingers, but leaves them all over the scene of the crime, the chances are about one in ten of finding a print that is sufficiently clear to be of any value.

21

The chief of police of a Southern city once gave me a description of a man, complete even to a mole on his neck, but neglected to mention that he had only one arm.

22

I know a forger who left his wife because she had learned to smoke cigarettes while he was serving a term in prison.

23

Second only to "Dr. Jekyll and Mr. Hyde" is "Raffles"* in the affections of the daily press. The phrase "gentleman crook" is used on the slightest provocation. A composite portrait of the gentry upon whom the newspapers have bestowed this title would show a laudanum-drinker, with a large rhinestone horseshoe aglow in the soiled bosom of his shirt below a bow tie, leering at his victim, and saying: "Now don't get scared, lady, I ain't gonna crack you on the bean. I ain't a rough-neck!"

24

The cleverest and most uniformly successful detective I have ever known is extremely myopic.

25

Going from the larger cities out into the remote rural communities, one finds a steadily decreasing percentage of crimes that have to do with money and a proportionate increase in the frequency of sex as a criminal motive.

26

While trying to peer into the upper story of a roadhouse in northern California one night—and the man I was looking for was in Seattle at the

---

* Gentleman burglar in the stories of E. W. Hornung, collected in *The Amateur Cracksman* (1895).

time—part of the porch roof crumbled under me and I fell, spraining an ankle. The proprietor of the roadhouse gave me water to bathe it in.

27

The chief difference between the exceptionally knotty problem confronting the detective of fiction and that facing the real detective is that in the former there is usually a paucity of clues, and in the latter altogether too many.

28

I know a man who once stole a Ferris-wheel.

29

That the law-breaker is invariably soon or late apprehended is probably the least challenged of extant myths. And yet the files of every detective bureau bulge with the records of unsolved mysteries and uncaught criminals.

≈≈≈

When life's greatest tragedies become its little ironies, we have learned to live.

≈≈≈

Every woman has two suitors—the man she loves and the one who amounts to something.

THE MAN WHO STOOD IN THE WAY

THE SENATOR kept biting his lip, as if he were beset with problems of insurmountable difficulty. He was a massive man, exuding an air of power. The spacious leather chair in which he sat seemed scarcely adequate for his weight; bulky shoulders and arms bulged over its sides with a suggestion of overflowing.

The Senator's head under his crisp mane of iron-gray hair was massive, too, and his features were large, cragged, and graven with the lines that indicate power.

When he arose presently and crossed the library to get whiskey and cigars for his guests, the immense room seemed to dwindle in an abrupt shrinking of wall and ceiling; and the polished floor threatened each instant to creak under the tread of his heavy feet, though it was far too genteel—as befit a floor in a Dupont Circle home—ever actually to creak. The vacated chair gaped wide, appeared, as the great upholstered cavern it really was, to lose its dignity immediately the Senator dropped into it again.

In marked contrast with the Senator was the man who sat stiffly upright on the edge of one of the room's least comfortable chairs and, ignoring the allure of the imported cigars his host had set at his elbow, employed a gnarled thumb to cram coarse, black tobacco into a yellow-gray corncob pipe.

He looked sixty-five, though he may have been ten years younger, and the years had served to parch rather than to mellow him. His unkempt hair, to the extent that it had survived, was a dingy yellow-white which had probably been sandy in its youth; a mustache of the same hue, except where tobacco had stained it a richer shade, straggled over withered lips. His forehead was low, narrow, and of an almost reptilian flatness; his nose was long and pinched and drooping below flat, lusterless eyes of a faded, unrecognizable color; his chin was frankly receding.

In his thick-soled boots he would have stood less than five and a half feet—say, just a trifle above the Senator's shoulder—and the beam of scales set at a hundred and five pounds would have been undisturbed by his presence. He wore a baggy suit of a once-snuff color, and a soft black hat lay on the floor beside his chair.

The pipe loaded, he turned to the table, filled a glass from the bottle, and drained it with neither the shudder nor the appreciative grimace which usually accompanies the drinking of straight whiskey. Then, disregarding the matches on the stand beside him, he felt in the pockets of his vest, brought out a match with the common brown head so seldom seen nowadays, ignited it sputteringly on the sole of a boot, and lighted his pipe.

His glance never for an instant rested on any of the furnishings of the luxurious room; it ranged from the Senator to the pipe, to the hat on the floor, and then back to the Senator.

Obviously unused to the elegance in which he now found himself, that little man was not comfortable, not at home; but his attitude was certainly not one of awe—rather he seemed to disapprove of the sybaritic apartment, and, disapproving, to ignore it altogether.

The Senator chewed a cigar, frowned at his feet, and talked. He was counted in political circles a reticent man, one who expressed himself crisply and concisely, with a great economy of words. But his conversation now was at variance with that reputation.

He talked desultorily, letting his sentences lose themselves half-formed, their logical endings being replaced by irrelevancies or not at all. The little man answered now and then with drawled monosyllables in a dry, reedy voice; he was plainly not engrossed by his host's words. It was clear that the Senator had not sent for him to discuss crops and the political situation in Sudlow County.

The Senator wasted three-quarters of an hour in this nervous dalliance. Then he threw his cold cigar into the fireplace and slid his chair forward to within a foot of his guest's. He leaned still closer, the lines between his eyebrows deepening.

"But all this isn't what I wanted to see you for, Inch," he said, his deep voice impressive even in its half-whisper. "I am in trouble. I need help."

Gene Inch nodded his head slightly.

"Can I count on you?" And then, as the meaningless nod came again, "You know I pardoned Tom when I was governor."

It was true enough that the impetus behind that pardoning had been political expediency; but what of it? He had pardoned Tom Inch.

Gene Inch took the pipe from his mouth and said: "Yeah, I know you pardoned Tom. You don't have to remind a Inch of his debts."

"You'll help me, then?"

"Uh-huh. Who do you want killed?"

The Senator quailed.

"Killed?" he repeated in a tone of horror. "Killed?"

Inch bared his stained and broken teeth in an evil grin.

"I hope it ain't no worse than that," he said. "But supposing you tell me what's what."

The Senator laid an unsteady hand on the other's bony knee.

"I'm being blackmailed. It has been going on for years, since shortly after I came to Sudlow County. All the years I was in the State legislature, when I was governor, and now since I have been senator, I have been paying—paying more and more every year. And now—now I've got to stop it. Inch, I have made a lot of friends since I have been here in Washington, and they are talking of running me for President. But I can't go ahead unless I shake this blackmailer off. I *must* shake him off, or I am stopped! The more prominent I become, the more insolent he is—it strengthens his hand just that much more—and if I should be elected President of this country. . . . I can't even try unless I get rid of him!"

Inch's face hadn't lighted up at mention of either the black-mailer or the Senator's presidential hopes, and his eyes were as void of fire as ever.

"Where'll I find this fellow?" he asked laconically.

"Wait, Gene," the Senator said. "We must be careful. There must be no scandal or my position will be even worse than now. I want you to fix it so he won't bother me, but I don't want anything done that will bring on worse trouble."

Inch let a shade of his contempt for this nicety show in the lift of his lips, and then he said:

"Well, I reckon you better tell me more about it, then."

The Senator's eyes narrowed. He spoke aloud, but more to himself than to his guest:

"I pardoned your boy Tom when he was serving life for killing Dick Haney. . . . All right!

"I came to Sudlow County nearly twenty years ago, remember? Well, I came there after escaping from the California State prison at San Quentin. I got in a fight in Oakland one night and killed a man. I wasn't known in Oakland and I gave a false name when I was arrested. I took my real name again after I escaped—I don't know of anybody else who ever did it from there. I was sentenced to thirty years, but after a year and a half I escaped. About two years after I had settled in Sudlow County a man who had been in San Quentin with me recognized me. Frank McPhail was his name, but he goes by the name of Henry Bush now. I've been pay-ing him every cent I could scrape together ever since."

Inch twisted the end of his long nose reflectively.

"Any chance of facing it down? I mean, can he prove anything?"

"The fingerprints—they are still on file at San Quentin."

"Do you reckon there's anybody in on it besides this Bush?"

The Senator shook his head.

"I am reasonably certain that he hasn't told anyone else"—bitterly—"or I should have heard from them, too."

"Where does this Bush live at? And what does he look like?"

"Wait, Gene!" the Senator pleaded. "You can't walk up and shoot him. He is well known here in Washington, and he is known to be a friend of mine—he has boasted enough of our intimacy! No matter how careful you are, if you kill him something would leak out, and I'd be worse off than I am now. And, besides, I can't stomach murder!"

Inch tweaked his nose thoughtfully again and focused his flat eyes on the dirty bowl of his pipe.

"What's the next nearest city to here?" he asked.

"Baltimore is only forty miles away."

"Do you reckon this Bush is known much in Baltimore?'

"I don't think he is. Why?"

Inch thrust the pipe into his pocket and picked up his hat.

"I'll see you tomorrow," he said.

The following evening Gene Inch called upon the Senator again. He stayed but a few minutes, talking to the Senator in the reception hall.

"You tell this Bush you want him to come see you tomorrow in Baltimore; that you'll be waiting for him in Room 411 at the Strand Hotel between ten and eleven at night; that he's to come right up to the room and not ask for you at the desk, because you ain't going to be registered under your own name. Can you make him swallow it?"

"I think so," the Senator said hesitantly, "but he'll be suspicious and come prepared for trouble. What are you going to do, Gene? You aren't going to—"

"You leave me be," Inch said querulously. "I'm going to fix this thing. Do as I tell you. It don't make no difference what he thinks, or how suspicious he is, get him over there and I'll get you out of your troubles."

The Senator's muscular hand shook as he opened the door for his caller; the skinny hand that pulled Inch's black hat down on his head was as steady as a Sudlow County boulder.

A dim light from the corridor entered Room 411 through the transom; through the closed window came a faint glow from the street lights; the two diluted the darkness in the room to an artificial, bluish twilight.

Gene Inch sat on a chair in a corner near the door, facing the door. He wore a suit of coarse, heavy underwear, which bulged in ill-fitting folds here and there over his angular figure.

Clamped between his teeth was the stem of a cold pipe; a battered and scratched revolver of heavy caliber hung from one hand. His bare feet were flat on the carpeted floor in an attitude of patient ease.

A clock somewhere struck ten. Twenty minutes passed. Then the knob of the unlocked door turned, the door opened, and a burly figure stood in the doorway. A black automatic pistol held high against the figure's chest pointed into the room.

The muzzle of Inch's revolver slid forward and nudged the side of the burly man. The latter's muscles jumped suddenly, but his feet did not move. Slowly his right hand opened and the automatic thudded dully on the floor.

Inch stepped back and said: "Come in and close the door behind you."

Then he motioned his captive to a chair and sat on the bed.

"You're Bush, I reckon."

"Yes, and if you think—"

"Shut your mouth and listen!"

Bush subsided before the menace in the reedy voice of this queer little man in ridiculous clothes who squinted wickedly at him in the dusk over the barrel of the enormous revolver.

"Take off your coat."

Bush obeyed.

"Throw it on the foot of the bed."

Bush hesitated. It might be possible to fling the coat at this old man's head and close with him. But, his eyes now accustomed to the dim light, he saw that the withered finger around the trigger held it back against the grip—the cocked hammer was restrained only by the pressure of the thumb. That pressure removed, the hammer would fall. Gently Bush tossed his coat to the bed. Inch went through the pockets with his left hand, removing everything. Then he threw the coat on the floor.

"Turn out your other pockets."

Bush emptied the pockets of his trousers and waistcoat: a knife, some keys, a few coins, a roll of paper money, a watch, a handkerchief.

"This suit is tailor-made, huh?" Inch said. "Then there had ought to be labels on the pants and vest as well as the coat. Take the knife and rip 'em all out. Give me your hat."

While the puzzled blackmailer—not yet suspecting his captor's intention—removed all the markings from his clothes Inch examined the hat. No initials were in it.

"Put on your coat and hat," he ordered. "Now put all them things back in your pocket except them bills, and your watch. You can drop the labels on the floor. Now stand back against the wall."

Inch picked up the roll of paper money and put it in the pocket of his trousers, which hung over the back of a chair. The watch, the cloth labels, and the things he had taken from Bush's coat he rolled in a handkerchief and put in his valise.

"Say—" Bush began.

"Shut your mouth!" Inch snapped irritably.

Then the old man looked carefully around the room and chuckled with sour satisfaction. He backed to the bed and pulled the covers down with his free hand and got into the bed, the revolver still menacing the other. He pulled the white covers up across his chest, half-sitting, half-lying against the pillows. Then slowly he drew the revolver back toward his body. The muzzle cleared the edge of the covers and slid out of sight.

Bush's mouth hung slack, bewilderment filled his face. As the weapon disappeared beneath the covers he contracted his leg muscles in the first movement of a spring. Before he could bend his knees in the second movement the room shook with a heavy explosion. A smoldering hole appeared on the white surface of the topsheet and grew rapidly larger. Bush toppled to the floor with blood seeping from a hole in his left breast. The room reeked with the blended odors of gunpowder and burning cloth.

Inch scrambled out of bed, took a flashlight and a homemade black mask from a dresser drawer, and dropped them beside the dead man. Then he kicked the automatic pistol, which lay near the door, over near one lifeless hand.

Fifteen minutes later the hotel detective and a policeman were examining the remains of Henry Bush, and listening to Gene Inch's story of retiring early, waking to see a man bending over the chair on which his clothes hung, carefully drawing his revolver from under the pillow, being surprised in that act by the burglar, and having to shoot through the bedcovers.

The detective and the patrolman finished their examination and conferred.

"Nothing to identify him by."

"No; not even a watch or anything we could trace."

"No use trying to trace the gun. Burglars don't get 'em that way."

The policeman turned to Inch.

"Come down to headquarters in the morning—about ten o'clock."

And then, admiringly: "You sure hit him pretty for having to shoot through them bedclothes!"

"The Senator is not in," said the girl in the outer office.

"Now, sister, you tell him Gene Inch wants to see him."

"But he—"

"Run along and tell him, sister."

The Senator came to the door of his private office to receive Inch and to usher him in. The Senator's face was pallid and he seemed to be having trouble with his breathing. The eyes that met Inch's held a strange mixture of hope and fear.

When they were alone in the private office Inch nodded.

"It's all done. Everything is all right."

"And he—"

"I seen by the papers where an unidentified burglar was killed trying to rob a farmer in a Baltimore hotel."

The Senator relaxed into a chair with a sobbing breath.

"Are you positive, Gene, that there can be no slip-up?"

Inch clucked scornfully.

"Ain't nothing can happen."

The Senator got to his feet and stretched out both hands to his savior.

"I can't ever pay you in full for what you have done, Gene, but no matter—"

Inch turned his rounded back upon the other's gratitude and walked to the door. With one hand on the knob he turned, leered malevolently at the Senator, and said:

"I'll expect a check on the first of every month; and I hope you get to be President—it'll mean a lot to me."

For a long space the Senator stood staring dumbly into the little man's flat, lifeless eyes. Then comprehension came to him. His knees sagged and he crumpled into his chair.

"But, Gene—"

"*But* hell!" Inch snarled. "The first of every month!"

THE JOKE ON ELOISE MOREY

"BUT, GOOD God, Eloise, I love you!"

"But, good God, Dudley, I hate you!"

The cold malevolence of her mimicry brought a quiver to his lips, as she knew it would, and his tortured face went altogether bloodless. These not unfamiliar, and in this case anticipated, indications of pain infuriated her even as they pleased her. From her advantage of perhaps two inches in height she let her hard gray eyes—twin points of steel in a beautiful, selfish face—range with studied insult from the wave of chestnut hair that swept over his forehead to the toes of his small shoes, and then up again to his suffering red-brown eyes.

"What are you?" she asked with frigid bitterness. "You're not a man; are you a child? or an insect? or what? You know I don't want you—you'll never be anything. I've certainly made that clear enough. And yet you won't give me my liberty. I wish I never had seen you—that I'd never married you—that you were dead!"

Her voice—she usually took pains to keep it carefully modulated—rose high and shrill under the pressure of her wrath.

Her husband winced under the lash of each scornful word, but said nothing. His was too sensitive a nature to permit of any of the answers he might have made. Where a cruder man would have met the woman on her own ground and hammered his way to victory, or at least an even distribution of the honors, he was helpless. As always, his silence, his helplessness, spurred her on to greater cruelties.

"An artist!" she derided, making the phrase heavy with contempt. "You were a genius; you were going to be famous and wealthy and God knows what all! And I fell for it and married you: a milk-and-water nincompoop who'll never be anything. An artist! An artist who paints pictures that nobody will look at, much less buy. Pictures that are supposed to be delicate. Delicate! Weak and wishy-washy daubs of color that are like the fool who paints them. A silly fool smearing paint on canvas—too fine for commercial art—too fine for anything! Twelve years you've spent learning to paint and can't turn out a picture anybody will look at twice! Great! You're great now; a great big fool!"

She paused to consider the effect of her tirade. It was indeed worthy of her oratory. Dudley Morey's knees shook, his head hung, his abject eyes were on the floor, and tears coursed down his pale cheeks.

"Get out!" she cried. "Get out of my room, before I kill you!"

He turned and stumbled through the doorway.

Alone, she raged up and down the room with the cushioned step of a panther. Her lips were drawn back, revealing small, even teeth; her fists were clenched; her eyes burned with an intensity more eloquent than the tears that never came to them could have been. For fifteen minutes she paced the floor. Then she flung open a closet door, caught up the first coat that came to her hand, a hat, and left the room, the confines of which seemed too small to hold her anger.

The maid was in the hall, dusting the balustrade; she looked at her mistress's passionate face with stupid surprise. Eloise passed her without a word, hardly seeing her, and descended the stairs. At the front door she stopped suddenly. She remembered that when she had passed the library door she had seen a desk drawer standing open, and it had been the drawer in which

Dudley's revolver was kept. She went back to the library. The revolver was gone.

She bit her lip thoughtfully. Dudley must have taken the revolver. Would he really kill himself? He always had been morbidly sensitive, and he had courage enough, if it came down to that, even if he was such a failure—such a fool at puddling with his paints. His inability to encompass success of one sort or another was the result of inordinate sensitiveness rather than anything else; and, taunted sufficiently, that sensitiveness could easily drive him to self-destruction. Suppose it did? What then? Wouldn't she—But, no! As likely as not he would bungle it somehow, as he had bungled everything else, and there would be a lot of unpleasant publicity.

She decided to go to his studio at once. That was the only thing to do. She couldn't telephone; he had no telephone in the studio. If she arrived in time she would stop him; and perhaps his attempt, or the bare intent, could be used to win the divorce he had refused her. Lawyers were clever at twisting things like that around to their clients' advantage. And if she arrived too late—well, she would have done her part. She knew her husband too well to doubt that she would find him in his studio.

She left the house and boarded a street car. The line ran past the building in which he had his studio.

When she stepped from the car she found herself running toward the building. The studio was on the fourth floor and there were no elevators. She became excited as she climbed and her breath came with difficulty. The stairs seemed interminable. Finally she reached the top floor and turned down the corridor that led to Dudley's room. She was trembling now, and moisture stood out on her face and in the palms of her hands. She tried not to think of what she might see when she opened her husband's door. She came to the door and stopped, listening. No sound. Then she pushed the door open.

Her husband stood in the middle of the room, under the skylight, with his back to the door. His right arm was raised in an awkward position, the elbow level with his shoulder, his forearm bent stiffly toward his head. Even as she divined the import of the pose, and screamed, "Dud-ley!" the air vibrated with the force of the explosion. Dudley Morey rocked slowly, once forward, once backward, and then crumpled face down upon the bare floor.

Eloise crossed the room slowly; she felt surprisingly calm now that it was all over. Beside her husband she stopped; but she did not bend to touch the body; it was too repulsive in death for that. A hole gaped in one temple—ringed by a dark, burned area. The revolver had fallen over against the wall. He still wore his top-coat and gloves.

She turned away with a feeling of disgust; the sight sickened her. She went to a chair and sat down.

It was all over now.

On the table before her she saw an envelope addressed to her in Dudley's tiny handwriting. She tore it open.

Dear Eloise:

You are right, I suppose, about my being a failure. I can't give you up while I live—so I am doing the best I can for you. Between losing you and never succeeding in finding what I want in my painting, I can't think of anything to live for anyway. Don't think that I am bitter, or that I blame you for anything, dear. I love you,

Dudley

She read it through twice, her face flushing with chagrin. How like Dudley to leave this note to brand her as the cause for his death! Why could he not have shown some thought, some consideration of her position? It was fortunate that she had found it. What an idea it would have given anyone else! And then it would have got into the newspapers. As if she were responsible for his death!

She went to the old-fashioned, open fireplace, in which a feeble fire burned, and thrust the letter in. Then she remembered the envelope and consigned it to the flames, too.

Several men and an old woman—apparently a charwoman—were at the door, turning curious glances from the man on the floor to the woman beyond. They edged into the room, grew bolder, and crowded around Dudley's body. Some of them mentioned his name. A man whom Eloise knew—Harker, an illustrator and a friend of her husband's—came in, savagely routed the group around the dead man, and knelt beside him. Harker looked up and saw Eloise for the first time. He got to his feet, took her by the arm with gentle force, and led her to his studio, on the floor below. He made her lie on the couch, spread a blanket over her, and left her. He returned in a few minutes and sat silently in a chair across the room, sucking at a calabash pipe, and staring at the floor. She sat up, but he would not let her talk about her husband, for which she was grateful.

Someone knocked on the door and Harker called, "Come in."

A heavy, middle-aged man with a florid face and a bellicose black mustache came in. He did not seem to think it necessary to remove his hat, but his manner was polite enough, in a stolid way. He introduced himself as Detective Sergeant Murray, and questioned Eloise.

She told him that her husband had been worrying over his lack of success with his painting; that he had seemed especially distraught that morning; that after he had gone she found his revolver was missing; that, fearing the worst, she had come to his studio, arriving just as he shot himself.

The detective asked further questions in his callous but not unkindly, tone. She answered truthfully enough on the whole, though she told rather less than the complete truth here and there. Murray made no comment, and then turned his attention to Harker.

Harker had heard the shot, but was too engrossed with his work to pay immediate attention to it. Then the thought had intruded that the noise, which might have been made by something falling, had come from the vicinity of Morey's studio, and he had gone up to investigate. He said that Morey had seemed increasingly worried of late, but had never talked of himself or his affairs.

Murray left the room and returned after a few minutes accompanied by a man whom he introduced as "Byerly of the Bureau."

"You'll have to go down to headquarters, Mrs. Morey," Murray said with a deprecatory gesture. "Byerly'll show you what to do. Just red tape. Only take a few minutes."

Eloise left the building with Byerly. As he turned toward the corner past which the street-car line ran she suggested a taxicab. He telephoned from the corner drugstore, and a few minutes later they were climbing the gray steps of the City Hall. Byerly led her through a door marked *Pawn-Shop Detail* and gave her a chair.

"Just wait a couple minutes here," he said.

Time dragged past. Half an hour. An hour. Two hours.

The door opened and Murray came in, followed by Byerly and a little fat man with a sparse handful of white hair spread over a broad pink scalp. Byerly called the fat man "Chief" when he pulled up a chair for him. The fat man and Byerly sat on chairs facing Eloise. Murray sat on a desk.

"Have you got anything to say?" Murray asked carelessly.

Her eyebrows went up.

"I beg your pardon?"

"All right," Murray said without emotion. "Eloise Morey, you're arrested for the murder of your husband, and anything you say may be used against you."

"Murder!" she exclaimed, startled out of her poise.

"Exactly," Murray said.

Some measure of her assurance came back to her. She wanted to laugh, but instead she said haughtily, "Why, that's ridiculous!"

Murray leaned forward. "Is it?" he asked imperturbably. "Now listen. You and your husband ain't been on good terms for some time. This morning you had a row. You said you wished he was dead, and you threatened him. Your servant girl heard you. Then after he left she saw you rush out, all worked up, and she saw you go to the drawer where the gun was kept. And she looked in the drawer after you was gone and the gun was gone, too. Two people saw you going up toward your husband's studio looking pretty wild, and they heard a woman's voice—an angry voice—just before the shot. And you admit yourself that you were in the room when your husband died. How's that? Still ridiculous?"

She had the sensation of a heavy net closing about her.

"But people don't kill each other every time they have a little family quarrel—even if all you say were true. Murder is supposed to require a stronger urge than that, isn't it? And I told you about finding the revolver gone and trying to get to his studio in time to save him, didn't I?"

Murray shook his head.

"Oh, I've got the 'strong urge' all right, Mrs. Eloise Morey. I found a batch of hot love letters, signed Joe, in your room, and some of 'em are dated as recent as yesterday. And I find that your husband was set against divorce. And I also find that he's got a tidy bit of life insurance and an income of three or four thousand a year that you come into. I got enough motive all right."

Eloise struggled to keep her face composed—everything appeared to hinge upon that—but the threatening net seemed closer, and now it was not so much a net as a great smothering blanket. She closed her eyes for an instant, but it was not to be escaped that way. Rage burned within her. She stood up and her eyes glared into the three alert, impassively complacent faces before her. "You fools!" she cried. "You—"

She remembered the letter Dudley had left behind; the letter that would have told the truth unmistakably; the letter that would have cleared her in a twinkling, the letter she had burned in the fireplace.

She swayed, tears of despair came to the hard gray eyes Detective Sergeant Murray left his seat and caught her as she fell.

HOLIDAY

PAUL LEFT the post office carrying his monthly compensation check in its unmistakable narrow manila envelope with the mocking bold-faced instructions to postmasters should the addressee have died meanwhile, and hurried back along the wooden walk to his ward, intent upon catching the physician in charge before he left for the morning. The ward surgeon, a delicately plump man in khaki, with a mouth permanently puckered, perhaps by its habit of framing a mild, prolonged "oh" whenever, as not infrequently happened, he could not find the exactly adequate words, was just leaving his office.

"I'd like to go to town this afternoon," Paul said.

The doctor went back to his desk and reached for a pad of pass blanks. This was a matter of routine; suitable words came easily. "Have you been out this week?"

"No, sir."

The physician's pen scratched across paper and Paul turned away waving in the air—to dry the ink, there never was a blotter at hand—the slip which permitted Hetherwick, Paul, to be absent from the United States Public Health Service Hospital No. 64 from 11 A.M. to 11 P.M. for the purpose of going to San Diego.

In the city he went first to a bank and exchanged the check for eight ten-dollar bills; then he filled his pockets with cigarettes and cigars and bought a racing program, studying it carefully while he ate luncheon.

He rode to Tijuana on the rear seat of an automobile stage, tightly wedged between a hatchet-faced tout who chewed gum unrestingly all the way and a large, perspiring, too-pink-and-yellow woman under a wide, limp hat. For a brief moment just beyond National City the savory fragrance of citrus fruits came into the car; for the rest of the trip his nostrils were busy with the unblending odors of spearmint, a heavy strawberry-like perfume from the woman beside him, burning oil, and the hot dust that scorched his throat and lungs and kept him coughing.

He hurried through the gate at the race track and reached the betting ring just in time to place his bets on the first race: five dollars on "Step At a Time" to win and five to place. He watched the race from the rail in front of the paddock, leaning forward to peer nearsightedly at the horses. "Step At a Time" won easily and at the paying booths Paul received thirty-six dollars and some silver for his two colored tickets.

At the grandstand bar he drank a glass of whiskey, then, consulting the penciled notes on his program, he bet ten dollars on Beauvis to win the second race. Beauvis finished second. Paul was not disappointed; that had been pretty close. His selection in the third race finished far in the rear; he won twenty-some dollars on the fourth, won again on the fifth, plunged a little on the sixth and lost. Between races he drank whiskey at the grandstand bar.

He had fourteen dollars in his pockets when he left the race track. The Casino was closed; he got into a dusty jitney and was driven to the Old Town.

He walked the length of the dingy street—a street that no mood of esthetic yea-saying could ever gild—and entered a saloon far down on the left-hand side, one that he had never visited before. A large, heavily muscled woman—she could easily, he thought, have been a blood relative of the woman in the automobile—broke off the song she was shouting to the nearly empty bar, linked a powerful arm through one of his, and said, "Come on over and sit down with me, honey."

He let her lead him to a booth—feeling a perverse delight in her utter coarseness—where she sat leaning heavily against him, one hand on his knee. He wondered what it would be like to lie in the arms of such a monster: middle-aged, bull-throated, grotesquely masked, manifestly without sex.

"You stick with me, dearie," she was saying, the words rolling out with a mechanical volubility and an absence of any attempt at glibness that testified to their too-frequent employment, "and I'll treat you right. You'll be a lot better off than you'd be fooling around with some of them sluts up the road."

He smiled and nodded politely. A sub-harlot, he decided, holding out false promises of her monstrous body to bring about that stimulation of traffic in liquor for which she was employed: a paradox, a sort of burlesque perhaps on a more familiar feminine attitude. The liquor he had drunk had fuddled him pleasantly, had clouded his never keen sight—though his eyes glowed brighter than usual—and had softened his speech. He bought several more drinks, amused by the keenness with which she watched the waiter, making sure that she received her metal tokens—upon which her commission was computed—for each order of drinks, and the naked greed with which she seized whatever change the waiter laid on the table.

He wondered after a while how much money he had left; it couldn't be much, and he must save from this enormity sufficient to buy a drink or two for the girl with the amazing red hair at the Palace. He motioned the waiter away.

"I'm flat," he told the woman. "They took me at the track."

"Tough luck," she said, and began to grow restless.

"Run along and let me finish my drink," he suggested. She grew confidential. "I'd like to, but once we girls start drinking with a man the boss makes us stay with him until he leaves."

He chuckled with joyful appreciation—he called that a neat arrangement—and got just a little unsteadily to his feet. She went to the door with him. "Be sure and come see me next time." He chuckled again at that, and then he felt an obscure shame: not at having squandered his few remaining dollars upon her, but at letting her think him so easily taken in.

"You've got me all wrong," he assured her, seriously. "I don't mind letting you take me for a ten or so when it's all I've got. Ten isn't much money one way or the other. But don't think I'm coming down here with a roll to let you—" Suddenly he saw himself standing in the doorway trying to justify himself to this monstrosity. He broke off with a laugh and walked away.

The girl with the red hair was dancing with a fat youth in tweeds to the achievements of a ferocious three-man orchestra when Paul entered the Palace. He waited buying a drink for himself and one for a girl in soiled brown silk who had come over to his side and who kept saying over and over: "This is too good to be true! I been here a week and I can't believe it yet. Think of all this!" Her arm took in all the bottles behind which one wall was hidden.

The fat youth in tweeds disappeared presently and the girl with the red hair saw Paul, waited for his nod, and joined him.

"Hello."

"Hello."

They drank and he motioned toward the change the bartender had put before him. She took it with casual thanks.

"How's the game go?" he asked.

"Pretty soft! And with you?"

"Not so good," he cheerfully complained. "The track knocked me over for most of what I had this afternoon."

She smiled sympathetically and they stood drinking slowly, smiling now and then with a certain definite delight each into the other's face. The clamor of the place, its garishness, was softened, nearly shut off from him by the pinkish alcoholic haze through which he regarded the world. But the girl's face, hair, figure, were clear enough to him.

He was filled with a strange affection for her: an affection that, though it was personal enough, had nothing of desire in it. Drunk as he undoubtedly was he did not want her physically. For all her beauty and pull upon his heart she was a girl who "hustled drinks" in a border town. That she might be a virgin—there wasn't anything impossible about that unlikely hypothesis: her profession didn't preclude it, even compelled continence during working hours—made no difference. It wasn't even so much that she was tainted by the pawing of strange hands—she had a freshness that had withstood that—as that in some obscure way the desires of too many men had rendered her no longer quite desirable. If he ever turned to a woman of this particularly sordid world it would be to some such monster as the one down the street. Given a certain turn of temper, there would be a savage, ghoulish joy in her.

He signalled the bartender again. They emptied their glasses, and he told her, "Well, I'm going to run along. I've got just about the price of a meal left."

"Won't you dance with me before you go?"

"No," he said, a warm feeling of renunciation flooding him, "you run along and get a live one."

"I don't care whether you've got any money or not," she said gravely. And then, "Let me lend—"

He backed away shaking his head. "So long!"

The girl in soiled brown silk called out to him as he passed the end of the bar where she stood drinking with two men, "It's too good to be true!" He smiled courteous agreement and went out into the street.

He stood for a moment beside the door, leaning against the wall, looking at the hazy figures around him—servicemen from San Diego in the uniforms of three branches, tourists, thieves, people who defied classification, the Mexicans (special policemen, all of them, rumor said) standing along the curb, the dogs—tasting a melancholy disgust at the tawdriness of this place which he thought could so easily be a gay play-spot.

From the doorway of the saloon he had just left, a pale girl spoke listlessly: "Come on in and get happy."

He raised an arm in a doubtful gesture "Look at 'em," he ordered sadly, "a flock of—" He thrust his hands into his trouser pockets and walked down the street grinning. He'd make a damned fool of himself yet!

A rack of picture post cards in the window of a curio shop caught his eye. He went in and bought half a dozen. Five of them he sent to friends in Philadelphia and New York. Over the sixth he pondered for some time: he could think of lots of people to send it to but he couldn't remember their addresses. Finally he sent it to a former casual acquaintance whom he hadn't seen since before the war but whose address he remembered because it was 444 Fourth Avenue. He penciled the same message on all six cards: "They tell me the States have gone dry."

In the street again he searched his pockets and counted his resources: eighty-five cents in silver and two return tickets: one from Tijuana to San Diego and the other from there to the hospital.

A husky voice whined at his elbow: "Say, buddy, can you give me the price of a cup of coffee?"

Paul laughed. "Fifty-fifty," he cried. "I got eighty-five cents. You get forty and we match for the odd nickel." He spun a coin in the air and was elated to find he had won. In an alley entrance across the street a San Diego stage was loading; he went over to it and sat beside the driver. He slumped down in the seat, half dozing through the ride back to the city, while behind him a girl with an undeveloped body and too finely-drawn features sang a popular song in a thin, plaintive voice.

Leaving the stage at its terminus, Paul walked up the side of the plaza to Broadway and turned toward a lunchroom where his forty-five cents would buy him a meal of sorts. Passing the entrance of the Grant Hotel he found himself in the center of a cluster of people and looking into the most beautiful face he had ever seen. He did not know he was staring until the beautiful face's escort in the uniform of a petty officer whispered to him, with peculiar, threatening emphasis: "Like her looks?"

Paul went on down the street slowly, turning the query over in his mind, wondering just what would be the mental processes of a man who under those conditions would ask that question in just that tone. He thought of turning around, finding the couple, and staring at the woman again to see what the petty officer would say then. But, looking back, he could not see them, so he went on to the lunchroom.

He found a cigar in his pocket after he had eaten, and smoked it during the ride back to the hospital. The fog-laden air rushing into the automobile chilled him and kept him coughing almost continuously. He wished he had brought an overcoat.

ARSON PLUS

JIM TARR picked up the cigar I rolled across his desk, looked at the band, bit off an end, and reached for a match.

"Three for a buck," he said. "You must want me to break a *couple* of laws for you this time."

I had been doing business with this fat sheriff of Sacramento County for four or five years—ever since I came to the Continental Detective Agency's San Francisco office—and I had never known him to miss an opening for a sour crack; but it didn't mean anything.

"Wrong both times," I told him. "I get them for two bits each, and I'm here to do you a favor instead of asking for one. The company that insured Thornburgh's house thinks somebody touched it off."

"That's right enough, according to the fire department. They tell me the lower part of the house was soaked with gasoline, but the Lord knows how they could tell—there wasn't a stick left standing. I've got McClump working on it, but he hasn't found anything to get excited about yet."

"What's the layout? All I know is that there was a fire."

Tarr leaned back in his chair and bellowed:

"Hey, Mac!"

The pearl push buttons on his desk are ornaments so far as he is concerned. Deputy sheriffs McHale, McClump, and Macklin came to the door together—MacNab apparently wasn't within hearing.

"What's the idea?" the sheriff demanded of McClump. "Are you carrying a bodyguard around with you?"

The two other deputies, thus informed as to whom "Mac" referred this time, went back to their cribbage game.

"We got a city slicker here to catch our firebug for us," Tarr told his deputy. "But we got to tell him what it's all about first."

McClump and I had worked together on an express robbery several months before. He's a rangy, towheaded youngster of twenty-five or six, with all the nerve in the world—and most of the laziness.

"Ain't the Lord good to us?"

He had himself draped across a chair by now—always his first objective when he comes into a room.

"Well, here's how she stands: This fellow Thornburgh's house was a couple miles out of town, on the old county road—an old frame house. About midnight, night before last, Jeff Pringle—the nearest neighbor, a half-mile or so to the east—saw a glare in the sky from over that way, and phoned in the alarm; but by the time the fire wagons got there, there wasn't enough of the house left to bother about. Pringle was the first of the neighbors to get to the house, and the roof had already fallen in then.

"Nobody saw anything suspicious—no strangers hanging around or nothing. Thornburgh's help just managed to save themselves, and that was all. They don't know much about what happened—too scared, I reckon. But they did see Thornburgh at his window just before the fire got him. A fellow here in town—name of Henderson—saw that part of it too. He was driving home from Wayton, and got to the house just before the roof caved in.

"The fire-department people say they found signs of gasoline. The Coonses, Thornburgh's help, say they didn't have no gas on the place. So there you are."

"Thornburgh have any relatives?"

"Yeah. A niece in San Francisco—a Mrs. Evelyn Trowbridge. She was up yesterday, but there wasn't nothing she could do, and she couldn't tell us nothing much, so she went back home."

"Where are the servants now?"

"Here in town. Staying at a hotel on I Street. I told 'em to stick around for a few days."

"Thornburgh own the house?"

"Uh-huh. Bought it from Newning & Weed a couple months ago."

"You got anything to do this morning?"

"Nothing but this."

"Good. Let's get out and dig around."

We found the Coonses in their room at the hotel on I Street. Mr. Coons was a small-boned, plump man with the smooth, meaningless face and the suavity of the typical male house-servant.

His wife was a tall, stringy woman, perhaps five years older than her husband—say, forty—with a mouth and chin that seemed shaped for gossiping. But he did all the talking, while she nodded her agreement to every second or third word.

"We went to work for Mr. Thornburgh on the fifteenth of June, I think," he said, in reply to my first question. "We came to Sacramento, around the first of the month, and put in applications at the Allis Employment Bureau. A couple of weeks later they sent us out to see Mr. Thornburgh, and he took us on."

"Where were you before you came here?"

"In Seattle, sir, with a Mrs. Comerford; but the climate there didn't agree with my wife—she has bronchial trouble—so we decided to come to California. We most likely would have stayed in Seattle, though, if Mrs. Comerford hadn't given up her house."

"What do you know about Thornburgh ?"

"Very little, sir. He wasn't a talkative gentleman. He hadn't any business that I know of. I think he was a retired seafaring man. He never said he was, but he had that manner and look. He never went out or had anybody in to see him, except his niece once, and he didn't write or get any mail. He had a room next to his bedroom fixed up as a sort of workshop. He spent most of his time in there. I always thought he was working on some kind of invention, but he kept the door locked, and wouldn't let us go near it."

"Haven't you any idea at all what it was?"

"No, sir. We never heard any hammering or noises from it, and never smelled anything either. And none of his clothes were ever the least bit soiled, even when they were ready to go out to the laundry. They would have been if he had been working on anything like machinery."

"Was he an old man?"

"He couldn't have been over fifty, sir. He was very erect, and his hair and beard were thick, with no gray hairs."

"Ever have any trouble with him?"

"Oh, no, sir! He was, if I may say it, a very peculiar gentleman in a way; and he didn't care about anything except having his meals fixed right, having his clothes taken care of—he was very particular about them—and not being disturbed. Except early in the morning and at night, we'd hardly see him all day."

"Now about the fire. Tell us everything you remember."

"Well, sir, my wife and I had gone to bed about ten o'clock, our regular time, and had gone to sleep. Our room was on the second floor, in the rear. Some time later—I never did exactly know what time it was—I woke up, coughing. The room was all full of smoke, and my wife was sort of strangling. I jumped up, and dragged her down the back stairs and out the back door. "When I had her safe in the yard, I thought of Mr. Thornburgh, and tried to get back in the house; but the whole first floor was just flames. I ran around front then, to see if he had got out, but didn't see anything of him. The whole yard was as light as day by then. Then I heard him scream—a horrible scream, sir—I can hear it yet! And I looked up at his window—that was the front second-story room—and saw him there, trying to get out the window. But all the woodwork was burning, and he screamed again and fell back, and right after that the roof over his room fell in.

"There wasn't a ladder or anything that I could have put up to the window—there wasn't anything I could have done.

"In the meantime, a gentleman had left his automobile in the road, and come up to where I was standing; but there wasn't anything we could do—the house was burning everywhere and falling in here and there. So we went back to where I had left my wife, and carried her farther away from the fire, and brought her to—she had fainted. And that's all I know about it, sir." "Hear any noises earlier that night? Or see anybody hanging around?"

"No, sir."

"Have any gasoline around the place?"

"No, sir. Mr. Thornburgh didn't have a car."

"No gasoline for cleaning?"

"No, sir, none at all, unless Mr. Thornburgh had it in his workshop. When his clothes needed cleaning, I took them to town, and all his laundry was taken by the grocer's man, when he brought our provisions."

"Don't know anything that might have some bearing on the fire?"

"No, sir. I was surprised when I heard that somebody had set the house afire. I could hardly believe it. I don't know why anybody should want to do that. . . ."

"What do you think of them?" I asked McClump, as we left the hotel.

"They might pad the bills, or even go South with some of the silver, but they don't figure as killers in my mind."

That was my opinion, too; but they were the only persons known to have been there when the fire started except the man who had died. We went around to the Allis Employment Bureau and talked to the manager.

He told us that the Coonses had come into his office on June second, looking for work; and had given Mrs. Edward Comerford, 45 Woodmansee Terrace, Seattle, Washington, as reference. In reply to a letter—he always checked up the references of servants—Mrs. Comerford had written that the Coonses had been in her employ for a number of years, and had been "extremely satisfactory in every respect." On June thirteenth, Thornburgh had telephoned the bureau, asking that a man and his wife be sent out to keep house for him, and Allis sent out two couples he had listed. Neither couple had been employed by Thornburgh, though Allis considered them more desirable than the Coonses, who were finally hired by Thornburgh.

All that would certainly seem to indicate that the Coonses hadn't deliberately maneuvered themselves into the place, unless they were the luckiest people in the world—and a detective can't afford to believe in luck or coincidence, unless he has unquestionable proof of it.

At the office of the real-estate agents, through whom Thornburgh had bought the house—Newning & Weed—we were told that Thornburgh had come in on the eleventh of June, and had said that he had been told that the house was for sale, had looked it over, and wanted to know the price. The deal had been closed the next morning, and he had paid for the house with a check for $14,500 on the Seamen's Bank of San Francisco. The house was already furnished.

After luncheon, McClump and I called on Howard Henderson— the man who had seen the fire while driving home from Wayton. He had an office in the Empire Building, with his name and the title *Northern California Agent for Krispy Korn Krumbs* on the door. He was a big, careless-looking man of forty-five or so, with the professionally jovial smile that belongs to the traveling salesman.

He had been in Wayton on business the day of the fire, he said, and had stayed there until rather late, going to dinner and afterward playing pool with a grocer named Hammersmith—one of his customers. He had left Wayton in his machine, at about ten thirty, and set out for Sacramento. At Tavender he had stopped at the garage for oil and gas, and to have one of his tires blown up.

Just as he was about to leave the garage, the garage man had called his attention to a red glare in the sky, and had told him that it was probably from a fire somewhere along the old county road that paralleled the State road into Sacramento; so Henderson had taken the county road, and had arrived at the burning house just in time to see Thornburgh try to fight his way through the flames that enveloped him.

It was too late to make any attempt to put out the fire, and the man upstairs was beyond saving by then—undoubtedly dead even before the roof collapsed; so Henderson had helped Coons revive his wife, and stayed there watching the fire until it had burned itself out. He had seen no one on that county road while driving to the fire. . . .

"What do you know about Henderson?" I asked McClump, when we were on the street.

"Came here, from somewhere in the East, I think, early in the summer to open that breakfast-cereal agency. Lives at the Garden Hotel. Where do we go next?"

"We get a car, and take a look at what's left of the Thornburgh house."

An enterprising incendiary couldn't have found a lovelier spot in which to turn himself loose, if he looked the whole county over. Tree-topped hills hid it from the rest of the world, on three sides; while away from the fourth, an uninhabited plain rolled down to the river. The county road that passed the front gate was shunned by automobiles, so McClump said, in favor of the State Highway to the north.

Where the house had been was now a mound of blackened ruins. We poked around in the ashes for a few minutes—not that we expected to find anything, but because it's the nature of man to poke around in ruins.

A garage in the rear, whose interior gave no evidence of recent occupation, had a badly scorched roof and front, but was otherwise undamaged. A shed behind it, sheltering an ax, a shovel, and various odds and ends of gardening tools, had escaped the fire altogether. The lawn in front of the house, and the garden behind the shed—about an acre in all—had been pretty thoroughly cut and trampled by wagon wheels, and the feet of the firemen and the spectators.

Having ruined our shoeshines, McClump and I got back in our car and swung off in a circle around the place, calling at all the houses within a mile radius, and getting little besides jolts for our trouble.

The nearest house was that of Pringle, the man who had turned in the alarm; but he not only knew nothing about the dead man, he said he had never even seen him. In fact, only one of the neighbors had ever seen him: a Mrs. Jabine, who lived about a mile to the south.

She had taken care of the key to the house while it was vacant; and a day or two before he bought it, Thornburgh had come to her house, inquiring about the vacant one. She had gone over there with him and showed him through it, and he had told her that he intended buying it, if the price wasn't too high.

He had been alone, except for the chauffeur of the hired car in which he had come from Sacramento, and, save that he had no family, he had told her nothing about himself.

Hearing that he had moved in, she went over to call on him several days later—"just a neighborly visit"—but had been told by Mrs. Coons that he was not at home. Most of the neighbors had talked to the Coonses, and had got the impression that Thornburgh did not care for visitors, so they had let him alone. The Coonses were described as "pleasant enough to talk to when you meet them," but reflecting their employer's desire not to make friends.

McClump summarized what the afternoon had taught us as we pointed our car toward Tavender: "Any of these folks could have touched off the place, but we got nothing to show that any of 'em even knew Thornburgh, let alone had a bone to pick with him."

Tavender turned out to be a crossroads settlement of a general store and post office, a garage, a church, and six dwellings, about two miles from Thornburgh's place. McClump knew the storekeeper and postmaster, a scrawny little man named Philo, who stuttered moistly.

"I n-n-never s-saw Th-thornburgh," he said, "and I n-n-never had any m-mail for him. C-coons"—it sounded like one of these things butterflies come out of—"used to c-come in once a week to-to order groceries—they d-didn't have a phone. He used to walk in, and I'd s-send the stuff over in my c-c-car. Th-then I'd s-see him once in a while, waiting f-for the stage to S-s-sacra-mento."

"Who drove the stuff out to Thornburgh's?"

"M-m-my b-boy. Want to t-talk to him?"

The boy was a juvenile edition of the old man, but without the stutter. He had never seen Thornburgh on any of his visits, but his business had taken him only as far as the kitchen. He hadn't noticed anything peculiar about the place.

"Who's the night man at the garage?" I asked him.

"Billy Luce. I think you can catch him there now. I saw him go in a few minutes ago."

We crossed the road and found Luce.

"Night before last—the night of the fire down the road—was there a man here talking to you when you first saw it?"

He turned his eyes upward in that vacant stare which people use to aid their memory.

"Yes, I remember now! He was going to town, and I told him that if he took the county road instead of the State Road he'd see the fire on his way in."

"What kind of looking man was he?"

"Middle-aged—a big man, but sort of slouchy. I think he had on a brown suit, baggy and wrinkled."

"Medium complexion?"

"Yes."

"Smile when he talked?"

"Yes, a pleasant sort of fellow."

"Brown hair?"

"Yeah, but have a heart!" Luce laughed. "I didn't put him under a magnifying glass."

From Tavender we drove over to Wayton. Luce's description had fit Henderson all right, but while we were at it, we thought

64

we might as well check up to make sure that he had been coming from Wayton.

We spent exactly twenty-five minutes in Wayton; ten of them finding Hammersmith, the grocer with whom Henderson had said he dined and played pool: five minutes finding the proprietor of the pool room; and ten verifying Henderson's story. . . .

"What do you think of it now, Mac?" I asked, as we rolled back toward Sacramento.

Mac's too lazy to express an opinion, or even form one, unless he's driven to it; but that doesn't mean they aren't worth listening to, if you can get them.

"There ain't a hell of a lot to think," he said cheerfully. "Henderson is out of it, if he ever was in it. There's nothing to show that anybody but the Coonses and Thornburgh were there when the fire started—but there may have been a regiment there. Them Coonses ain't too honest-looking, maybe, but they ain't killers, or I miss my guess. But the fact remains that they're the only bet we got so far. Maybe we ought to try to get a line on them."

"All right," I agreed. "Soon as we get back to town, I'll get a wire off to our Seattle office asking them to interview Mrs. Comerford, and see what she can tell about them. Then I'm going to catch a train for San Francisco and see Thornburgh's niece in the morning."

Next morning, at the address McClump had given me—a rather elaborate apartment building on California Street—I had to wait three-quarters of an hour for Mrs. Evelyn Trowbridge to dress. If I had been younger, or a social caller, I suppose I'd have felt amply rewarded when she finally came in—a tall, slender woman of less than thirty; in some sort of clinging black affair; with a lot of black hair over a very white face, strikingly set off by a small red mouth and big hazel eyes.

But I was a busy, middle-aged detective, who was fuming over having his time wasted; and I was a lot more interested in finding the bird who struck the match than I was in feminine beauty.

However, I smothered my grouch, apologized for disturbing her at such an early hour, and got down to business.

"I want you to tell me all you know about your uncle—his family, friends, enemies, business connections—everything."

I had scribbled on the back of the card I had sent into her what my business was.

"He hadn't any family," she said, "unless I might be it. He was my mother's brother, and I am the only one of that family now living."

"Where was he born?"

"Here in San Francisco. I don't know the date, but he was about fifty years old, I think—three years older than my mother."

"What was his business?"

"He went to sea when he was a boy, and, so far as I know, always followed it until a few months ago."

"Captain?"

"I don't know. Sometimes I wouldn't see or hear from him for several years, and he never talked about what he was doing; though he would mention some of the places he had visited—Rio de Janeiro, Madagascar, Tobago, Christiania. Then, about three months ago—some time in May—he came here and told me that he was through with wandering; that he was going to take a house in some quiet place where he could work undisturbed on an invention in which he was interested.

"He lived at the Francisco Hotel while he was in San Francisco. After a couple of weeks he suddenly disappeared. And then, about a month ago, I received a telegram from him, asking me to come to see him at his house near Sacramento. I went up the very next day, and I thought that he was acting queerly—he seemed very excited over something. He gave me a will that he had just drawn up and some life-insurance policies in which I was beneficiary.

"Immediately after that he insisted that I return home, and hinted rather plainly that he did not wish me to either visit him again or write until I heard from him. I thought all that rather peculiar, as he had always seemed fond of me. I never saw him again."

"What was this invention he was working on ?"

"I really don't know. I asked him once, but he became so excited—even suspicious—that I changed the subject, and never mentioned it again."

"Are you sure that he really did follow the sea all those years?"

"No, I am not. I just took it for granted; but he may have been doing something altogether different."

"Was he ever married?"

"Not that I know of."

"Know any of his friends or enemies?"

"No, none."

"Remember anybody's name that he ever mentioned?"

"No."

"I don't want you to think this next question insulting, though I admit it is. Where were you the night of the fire?"

"At home; I had some friends here to dinner, and they stayed until about midnight. Mr. and Mrs. Walker Kellogg, Mrs. John Dupree, and a Mr. Killmer, who is a lawyer. I can give you their addresses, if you want to question them."

From Mrs. Trowbridge's apartment I went to the Francisco Hotel. Thornburgh had been registered there from May tenth to June thirteenth, and hadn't attracted much attention. He had been a tall, broad-shouldered, erect man of about fifty, with rather long brown hair brushed straight back; a short, pointed brown beard, and a healthy, ruddy complexion—grave, quiet, punctilious in dress and manner; his hours had been regular and he had had no visitors that any of the hotel employees remembered.

At the Seamen's Bank—upon which Thornburgh's check, in payment of the house, had been drawn—I was told that he had opened an account there on May fifteenth, having been introduced by W. W. Jeffers & Sons, local stockbrokers. A balance of a little more than four hundred dollars remained to his credit. The cancelled checks on hand were all to the order of various life-in-surance companies; and for amounts that, if they represented pre-miums, testified to rather large policies. I jotted down the names of the life-insurance companies, and then went to the offices of W. W. Jeffers & Sons.

Thornburgh had come in, I was told, on the tenth of May with $15,000 worth of bonds that he had wanted sold. During one of his conversations with Jeffers he had asked the broker to recommend a bank, and Jeffers had given him a letter of introduction to the Seamen's Bank.

That was all Jeffers knew about him. He gave me the numbers of the bonds, but tracing bonds isn't always the easiest thing in the world.

The reply to my Seattle telegram was waiting for me at the Continental Detective Agency when I arrived.

MRS. EDWARD COMERFORD RENTED APARTMENT AT ADDRESS
YOU GIVE ON MAY TWENTY-FIVE. GAVE IT UP JUNE SIX. TRUNKS
TO SAN FRANCISCO SAME DAY CHECK NUMBERS ON FOUR FIVE
TWO FIVE EIGHT SEVEN AND EIGHT AND NINE.

Tracing baggage is no trick at all, if you have the dates and check numbers to start with—as many a bird who is wearing somewhat similar numbers on his chest and back, because he overlooked that detail when making his getaway, can tell you—and twenty-five minutes in a baggage-room at the Ferry and half an hour in the office of a transfer company gave me my answer.

The trunks had been delivered to Mrs. Evelyn Trowbridge's apartment!

I got Jim Tarr on the phone and told him about it.

"Good shooting!" he said, forgetting for once to indulge his wit. "We'll grab the Coonses here and Mrs. Trowbridge there, and that's the end of another mystery."

"Wait a minute!" I cautioned him. "It's not all straightened out yet—there're still a few kinks in the plot."

"It's straight enough for me. I'm satisfied."

"You're the boss, but I think you're being a little hasty. I'm going up and talk with the niece again. Give me a little time before you phone the police here to make the pinch. I'll hold her until they get there."

Evelyn Trowbridge let me in this time, instead of the maid who had opened the door for me in the morning, and she led me to the same room in which we had had our first talk. I let her pick out a seat, and then I selected one that was closer to either door than hers was.

On the way up I had planned a lot of innocent-sounding questions that would get her all snarled up; but after taking a good look at this woman sitting in front of me, leaning comfortably back in her chair, coolly waiting for me to speak my piece, I discarded the trick stuff and came out cold-turkey.

"Ever use the name Mrs. Edward Comerford?"

"Oh, yes." As casual as a nod on the street.

"When?"

"Often. You see, I happen to have been married not so long ago to Mr. Edward Comerford. So it's not really strange that I should have used the name."

"Use it in Seattle recently?"

"I would suggest," she said sweetly, "that if you are leading up to the references I gave Coons and his wife, you might save time by coming right to it."

"That's fair enough," I said. "Let's do that."

There wasn't a tone or shading, in voice, manner, or expression, to indicate that she was talking about anything half so serious or important to her as a possibility of being charged with murder. She might have been talking about the weather.

"During the time that Mr. Comerford and I were married, we lived in Seattle, where he still lives. After the divorce, I left Seattle and resumed my maiden name. And the Coonses were in our employ, as you might learn if you care to look it up. You'll find my husband—or former husband—at the Chelsea Apartments, I think.

"Last summer, or late spring, I decided to return to Seattle. The truth of it is—I suppose all my personal affairs will be aired anyhow—that I thought perhaps Edward and I might patch up our differences; so I went back and took an apartment on Woodmansee Terrace. As I was known in Seattle as Mrs. Edward Comerford, and as I thought my using his name might influence him a little, I used it while I was there.

"Also I telephoned the Coonses to make tentative arrangements in case Edward and I should open our house again; but Coons told me that they were going to California, and so I gladly gave them an excellent recommendation when, some days later, I received a letter of inquiry from an employment bureau in Sacramento. After I had been in Seattle for about two weeks, I changed my mind about the reconciliation—Edward's interest, I learned, was all centered elsewhere; so I returned to San Francisco—"

"Very nice! But—"

"If you will permit me to finish," she interrupted. "When I went to see my uncle in response to his telegram, I was surprised to find the Coonses in his house. Knowing my uncle's peculiarities, and finding them now increased, and remembering his extreme secretiveness about his mysterious invention, I cautioned the Coonses not to tell him that they had been in my employ.

"He certainly would have discharged them, and just as certainly would have quarreled with me—he would have thought that I was having him spied on. Then, when Coons telephoned me after the fire, I knew that to admit that the Coonses had been formerly in my employ, would, in view of the fact that I was my uncle's only heir, cast suspicion on all three of us. So we foolishly agreed to say nothing and carry on the deception."

That didn't sound all wrong—but it didn't sound all right. I wished Tarr had taken it easier and let us get a better line on these people, before having them thrown in the coop.

"The coincidence of the Coonses stumbling into my uncle's house is, I fancy, too much for your detecting instincts," she went on. "Am I to consider myself under arrest?"

I'm beginning to like this girl; she's a nice, cool piece of work.

"Not yet," I told her. "But I'm afraid it's going to happen pretty soon."

She smiled a little mocking smile at that, and another when the doorbell rang.

It was O'Hara from police headquarters. We turned the apartment upside down and inside out, but didn't find anything of importance except the will she had told me about, dated July eighth, and her uncle's life-insurance policies. They were all dated between May fifteenth and June tenth, and added up to a little more than $200,000.

I spent an hour grilling the maid after O'Hara had taken Evelyn Trowbridge away, but she didn't know any more than I did. However, between her, the janitor, the manager of the apartments, and the names Mrs. Trowbridge had given me, I learned that she had really been entertaining friends on the night of the fire—until after eleven o'clock, anyway—and that was late enough.

Half an hour later I was riding the Short Line back to Sacramento. I was getting to be one of the line's best customers, and my anatomy was on bouncing terms with every bump in the road.

Between bumps I tried to fit the pieces of this Thornburgh puzzle together. The niece and the Coonses fit in somewhere, but not just where we had them. We had been working on the job sort of lopsided, but it was the best we could do with it. In the beginning we had turned to the Coonses and Evelyn Trowbridge because there was no other direction to go; and now we had something on them—but a good lawyer could make hash out of it.

The Coonses were in the county jail when I got to Sacramento. After some questioning they had admitted their connection with the niece, and had come through with stories that matched hers.

Tarr, McClump and I sat around the sheriff's desk and argued.

"Those yarns are pipe dreams," the sheriff said. "We got all three of 'em cold, and they're as good as convicted."

McClump grinned derisively at his superior, and then turned to me.

"Go on, you tell him about the holes in his little case. He ain't your boss, and can't take it out on you later for being smarter than he is!"

Tarr glared from one of us to the other.

"Spill it, you wise guys!" he ordered.

"Our dope is," I told him, figuring that McClump's view of it was the same as mine, "that there's nothing to show that even Thornburgh knew he was going to buy that house before the tenth of June, and that the Coonses were in town looking for work on the second. And besides, it was only by luck that they got the jobs. The employment office sent two couples out there ahead of them."

"We'll take a chance on letting the jury figure that out."

"Yes? You'll also take a chance on them figuring out that Thornburgh, who seems to have been a nut, might have touched off the place himself! We've got something on these people, Jim, but not enough to go into court with them. How are you going to prove that when the Coonses were planted in Thornburgh's house—if you can even prove that they were planted—they and the Trowbridge woman knew he was going to load up with insurance policies?"

The sheriff spat disgustedly.

"You guys are the limit! You run around in circles, digging up the dope on these people until you get enough to hang 'em, and then you run around hunting for outs! What's the matter with you now?"

I answered him from halfway to the door—the pieces were beginning to fit together under my skull.

"Going to run some more circles—come on, Mac!"

McClump and I held a conference on the fly, and then I got a car from the nearest garage and headed for Tavender. We made time going out, and got there before the general store had closed for the night. The stuttering Philo separated himself from the two men with whom he had been talking Hiram Johnson,* and followed me to the rear of the store.

"Do you keep an itemized list of the laundry you handle?"

"N-n-no; just the amounts."

"Let's look at Thornburgh's."

He produced a begrimed and rumpled account book, and we picked out the weekly items I wanted: $2.60, $3.10, $2.25, and so on.

"Got the last batch of laundry here?"

"Y-yes," he said. "It j-just c-c-came out from the city t-today."

I tore open the bundle—some sheets, pillowcases, tablecloths, towels, napkins; some feminine clothing; some shirts, collars, underwear, and socks that were unmistakably Coons's. I thanked Philo while running back to the car.

Back in Sacramento again, McClump was waiting for me at the garage where I had hired the car.

"Registered at the hotel on June fifteenth; rented the office on the sixteenth. I think he's in the hotel now," he greeted me.

We hurried around the block to the Garden Hotel.

"Mr. Henderson went out a minute or two ago," the night clerk told us. "He seemed to be in a hurry."

"Know where he keeps his car?"

"In the hotel garage around the corner."

We were within ten feet of the garage, when Henderson's automobile shot out and turned up the street.

"Oh, Mr. Henderson!" I cried, trying to keep my voice level.

He stepped on the gas and streaked away from us.

"Want him?" McClump asked; and at my nod he stopped a passing roadster by the simple expedient of stepping in front of it.

We climbed in, McClump flashed his star at the bewildered driver, and pointed out Henderson's dwindling tail-light. After he had persuaded himself that he wasn't being boarded by a couple of bandits, the commandeered driver did his best, and we picked

---

* Governor of California (1911–17) and Theodore Roosevelt's running mate on the Progressive ticket in 1912.

up Henderson's tail-light after two or three turnings, and closed in on him—though his car was going at a good clip.

By the time we reached the outskirts of the city, we had crawled up to within safe shooting distance, and I sent a bullet over the fleeing man's head. Thus encouraged, he managed to get a little more speed out of his car; but we were overhauling him now.

Just at the wrong minute Henderson decided to look over his shoulder at us—an unevenness in the road twisted his wheels—his machine swayed—skidded—went over on its side. Almost immediately, from the heart of the tangle, came a flash and a bullet moaned past my ear. Another. And then, while I was still hunting for something to shoot at in the pile of junk we were drawing down upon, McClump's ancient and battered revolver roared in my other ear. Henderson was dead when we got to him—McClump's bullet had taken him over one eye. McClump spoke to me over the body.

"I ain't an inquisitive sort of fellow, but I hope you don't mind telling me why I shot this lad."

"Because he was—*Thornburgh.*"

He didn't say anything for about five minutes. Then: "I reckon that's right. How'd you know it?"

We were sitting beside the wreckage now, waiting for the police that we had sent our commandeered chauffeur to phone for.

"He had to be," I said, "when you think it all over. Funny we didn't hit on it before! All that stuff we were told about Thornburgh had a fishy sound. Whiskers and an unknown profession, immaculate and working on a mysterious invention, very secretive and born in San Francisco—where the fire wiped out all the old records—just the sort of fake that could be cooked up easily.

"Now, consider Henderson. You had told me he came to Sacramento sometime early this summer—and the dates you got tonight show that he didn't come until after Thornburgh had bought his house. All right! Now compare Henderson with the descriptions we got of Thornburgh.

"Both are about the same size and age, and with the same color hair. The differences are all things that can be manufactured—clothes, a little sunburn, and a month's growth of beard, along with a little acting, would do the trick. Tonight I went out to Tavender and took a look at the last batch of laundry—*and there wasn't any that didn't fit the Coonses!* And none of the bills all the way back were large enough for Thornburgh to have been as careful about his clothes as we were told he was."

"It must be great to be a detective!" McClump grinned as the police ambulance came up and began disgorging policemen. "I reckon somebody must have tipped Henderson off that I was asking about him this evening." And then, regretfully: "So we ain't going to hang them folks for murder after all."

"No, but we oughtn't have any trouble convicting them of arson plus conspiracy to defraud, and anything else that the Prosecuting Attorney can think up."

IN THE MORGUE

WALTER DOWE took the last sheet of the manuscript from his typewriter with a satisfied sigh and leaned back in his chair, turning his face to the ceiling to ease the stiffened muscles of his neck. Then he looked at the clock: 3:15 A.M. He yawned, got to his feet, switched off the lights, and went down the hall to his bedroom. In the doorway of the bedroom he halted abruptly. The moonlight came through the wide windows to illuminate an empty bed. He turned on the lights and looked around the room. None of the things his wife had worn that night were there. She had not undressed, then; perhaps she had heard the rattle of his typewriter and had decided to wait downstairs until he had finished. She never interrupted him when he was at work, and he was usually too engrossed by his labors to hear her footsteps when she passed his study door.

He went to the head of the stairs and called: "Althea!"

No answer.

He went downstairs, into all the rooms, turning on the lights; he returned to the second floor and did the same. His wife was not in the house. He was perplexed, and a little helpless. Then he remembered that she had gone to the theater with the Schuylers. His hands trembled as he picked up the telephone.

The Schuylers' maid answered his call . . . There had been a fire at the Majestic Theater; neither Mr. nor Mrs. Schuyler had come home. Mr. Schuyler's father had gone out to look for them, but had not returned yet. The maid understood that the fire had been pretty bad . . .

Dowe was waiting on the sidewalk when the taxicab for which he had telephoned arrived. Fifteen minutes later he was struggling to get through the fire lines, which were still drawn about the theater. A perspiring, red-faced policeman thrust him back.

"You'll find nothing here. The building's been cleared. Everybody's been taken to the hospitals."

Dowe found his cab again and was driven to the City Hospital. He forced his way through the clamoring group on the gray stone steps. A policeman blocked the door. Presently a pasty-faced man, in solid white, spoke over the policeman's shoulder:

"There's no use waiting. We're too busy treating them now to either take their names or let anybody in to see them. We'll try to have a list in the late morning edition; but we can't let anybody in until later in the day."

Dowe turned away. Then he thought: Murray Bornis, of course! He went back to the cab and gave the driver Bornis's address.

Bornis came to the door of his apartment in pajamas. Dowe clung to him.

"Althea went to the Majestic tonight and hasn't come home. They wouldn't let me in at the hospital. Told me to wait—but I can't! You're the police commissioner—you can get me in!"

While Bornis dressed, Dowe paced the floor, babbling. Then he caught a glimpse of himself in a mirror, and stood suddenly still.

The sight of his distorted face and wild eyes shocked him back into sanity. He was on the verge of hysterics. He must take hold of himself. He must not collapse before he found Althea.

Deliberately, he made himself sit down, made himself stop visualizing Althea's soft, white body charred and crushed. He must think about something else: Bornis, for instance . . .

But that brought him back to his wife in the end. She had never liked Bornis. His frank sensuality, and his unsavory reputation for numerous affairs with numerous women, had offended her strict conception of morality. To be sure, she had always given him all the courtesy due her husband's friend; but it was generally a frigid giving. And Bornis, understanding her attitude, and perhaps a little contemptuous of her narrow views, had been as coolly polite as she. And now she was lying somewhere, moaning in agony, perhaps already cold . . .

Bornis finished dressing and they went quickly to the City Hospital, where the police commissioner and his companion were readily admitted. They walked down long rooms, between rows of groaning and writhing bodies, looking into bruised and burned faces, seeing no one they knew. Then to Mercy Hospital where they found Sylvia Schuyler. She told them that the crush in the theater had separated her from her husband and Althea, and she had not seen them afterward. Then she lapsed into unconsciousness again.

When they got back to the cab, Bornis gave directions to the driver in an undertone, but Dowe did not have to hear them to know what they were: "To the morgue." There was no other place to go.

Now they walked between rows of bodies that were mangled horribly. Dowe had exhausted his feelings: he felt no pity, no loathing, now. He looked into a face; it was not Althea's; then it was nothing; he passed on to the next.

Bornis's fingers closed convulsively around Dowe's arm.

"There! Althea!"

Dowe turned. A face that stampeding leather heels had robbed of features; a torso that was battered and blackened and cut, and from which the clothing had been torn. All that was human of it were the legs; they had somehow escaped disfigurement.

"No, no!" Dowe cried.

He would not believe this begrimed, mangled thing was exquisite white Althea!

Through the horror that for the moment shut Dowe off from the world, Bornis's vibrant, anguished voice penetrated—it was almost a shriek:

"I tell you it is!" Flinging out a hand to point at one smooth knee. "See! The dimple!"

THE GATEWOOD CAPER

HARVEY GATEWOOD had issued orders that I was to be admitted as soon as I arrived, so it took me only a little less than fifteen minutes to thread my way past the doorkeepers, office boys, and secretaries who filled up most of the space between the Gatewood Lumber Corporation's front door and the president's private office. His office was large, all mahogany and bronze and green plush, with a mahogany desk as big as a bed in the center of the floor.

Gatewood, leaning across the desk, began to bark at me as soon as the obsequious clerk who had bowed me in bowed himself out.

"My daughter was kidnaped last night! I want the____that did it if it takes every cent I got!"

"Tell me about it," I suggested.

But he wanted results, it seemed, and not questions, and so I wasted nearly an hour getting information that he could have given me in fifteen minutes.

He was a big bruiser of a man, something over 200 pounds of hard red flesh, and a czar from the top of his bullet head to the toes of his shoes that would have been at least number twelves if they hadn't been made to measure.

He had made his several millions by sandbagging everybody that stood in his way, and the rage he was burning up with now didn't make him any easier to deal with.

His wicked jaw was sticking out like a knob of granite and his

79

eyes were filmed with blood—he was in a lovely frame of mind. For a while it looked as if the Continental Detective Agency was going to lose a client, because I'd made up my mind that he was going to tell me all I wanted to know, or I'd chuck the job.

But finally I got the story out of him.

His daughter Audrey had left their house on Clay Street at about 7 o'clock the preceding evening, telling her maid that she was going for a walk. She had not returned that night—though Gatewood had not known that until after he had read the letter that came this morning.

The letter had been from someone who said that she had been kidnaped. It demanded $50,000 for her release, and instructed Gatewood to get the money ready in hundred dollar bills—so that there would be no delay when he was told the manner in which the money was to be paid over to his daughter's captors. As proof that the demand was not a hoax, a lock of the girl's hair, a ring she always wore, and a brief note from her, asking her father to comply with the demands, had been enclosed.

Gatewood had received the letter at his office and had telephoned to his house immediately. He had been told that the girl's bed had not been slept in the previous night and that none of the servants had seen her since she started out for her walk. He had then notified the police, turning the letter over to them; and a few minutes later he had decided to employ private detectives also.

"Now," he burst out, after I had wormed these things out of him, and he had told me that he knew nothing of his daughter's associates or habits, "go ahead and do something! I'm not paying you to sit around and talk about it!"

"What are you going to do?" I asked.

"Me? I'm going to put those____behind bars if it takes every cent I've got in the world!"

"Sure! But first you get that $50,000 ready, so you can give it to them when they ask for it."

He clicked his jaw shut and thrust his face into mine.

"I've never been clubbed into doing anything in my life! And I'm too old to start now!" he said. "I'm going to call these people's bluff!"

"That's going to make it lovely for your daughter. But, aside from what it'll do to her, it's the wrong play. Fifty thousand isn't a whole lot to you, and paying it over will give us two chances that we haven't got now. One when the payment is made—a chance either to nab whoever comes for it or get a line on them. And the other when your daughter is returned. No matter how careful they are, it's a cinch she'll be able to tell us something that will help us grab them."

He shook his head angrily, and I was tired of arguing with him. So I left, hoping he'd see the wisdom of the course I had advised before too late.

At the Gatewood residence I found butlers, second men, chauffeurs, cooks, maids, upstairs girls, downstairs girls, and a raft of miscellaneous flunkies—he had enough servants to run a hotel.

What they told me amounted to this: The girl had not received a phone call, note by messenger, or telegram—the time-honored devices for luring a victim out to a murder or abduction—before she left the house. She had told her maid that she would be back within an hour or two; but the maid had not been alarmed when her mistress failed to return all that night.

Audrey was the only child, and since her mother's death she had come and gone to suit herself. She and her father didn't hit it off very well together—their natures were too much alike, I gathered—and he never knew where she was. There was nothing unusual about her remaining away all night. She seldom bothered to leave word when she was going to stay overnight with friends.

She was nineteen years old, but looked several years older: about five feet five inches tall, and slender. She had blue eyes, brown hair—very thick and long—was pale and very nervous. Her photographs, of which I took a handful, showed that her eyes were large, her nose small and regular, and her chin pointed.

She was not beautiful, but in the one photograph where a smile had wiped off the sullenness of her mouth, she was at least pretty.

When she left the house she was wearing a light tweed skirt and jacket with a London tailor's labels in them, a buff silk shirtwaist with stripes a shade darker, brown wool stockings, low-heeled brown oxfords, and an untrimmed gray felt hat.

I went up to her rooms—she had three on the third floor—and looked through all her stuff. I found nearly a bushel of photographs of men, boys, and girls; and a great stack of letters of varying degrees of intimacy, signed with a wide assortment of names and nicknames. I made notes of all the addresses I found.

Nothing in her rooms seemed to have any bearing on her abduction, but there was a chance that one of the names and addresses might be of someone who had served as a decoy. Also, some of her friends might be able to tell us something of value.

I dropped in at the Agency and distributed the names and addresses among the three operatives who were idle, sending them out to see what they could dig up.

Then I reached the police detectives who were working on the case—O'Gar and Thode—by telephone, and went down to the Hall of Justice to meet them. Lusk, a post-office inspector, was also there. We turned the job around and around, looking at it from every angle, but not getting very far. We were all agreed, however, that we couldn't take a chance on any publicity, or work in the open, until the girl was safe.

They had had a worse time with Gatewood than I—he had wanted to put the whole thing in the newspapers, with the offer of a reward, photographs, and all. Of course, Gatewood was right in claiming that this was the most effective way of catching the kidnapers—but it would have been tough on his daughter if her captors happened to be persons of sufficiently hardened character. And kidnapers as a rule aren't lambs.

I looked at the letter they had sent. It was printed with pencil on ruled paper of the kind that is sold in pads by every stationery dealer in the world. The envelope was just as common, also addressed in pencil, and postmarked *San Francisco, September 20, 9 P.M.* That was the night she had been seized. The letter read:

Sir:

We have your charming daughter and place a value of $50,000 upon her. You will get the money ready in $100 bills at once so there will be no delay when we tell you how it is to be paid over to us.

We beg to assure you that things will go badly with your daughter should you not do as you are told, or should you bring the police into this matter, or should you do anything foolish.

$50,000 is only a small fraction of what you stole while we were living in mud and blood in France for you, and we mean to get that much or else!

Three.

A peculiar note in several ways. They are usually written with a great pretense of partial illiterateness. Almost always there's an attempt to lead suspicion astray. Perhaps the ex-service stuff was there for that purpose ... or perhaps not.

Then there was a postscript:

We know someone who will buy her even after we are through with her—in case you won't listen to reason.

The letter from the girl was written jerkily on the same kind of paper, apparently with the same pencil.

Daddy—

Please do as they ask! I am so afraid—

Audrey

A door at the other end of the room opened, and a head came through.

"O'Gar! Thode! Gatewood just called up. Get up to his office right away!"

The four of us tumbled out of the Hall of Justice and into a police car.

Gatewood was pacing his office like a maniac when we pushed aside enough hirelings to get to him. His face was hot with blood and his eyes had an insane glare in them.

"She just phoned me!" he cried thickly, when he saw us.

It took a minute or two to get him calm enough to tell us about it

"She called me on the phone. Said, 'Oh, Daddy! Do something! I can't stand this—they're killing me!' I asked her if she knew where she was, and she said, 'No, but I can see Twin Peaks from here. There's three men and a woman, and—' And then I heard a man curse, and a sound as if he had struck her, and the phone went dead. I tried to get central to give me the number, but she couldn't! It's a damned outrage the way the telephone system is run. We pay enough for service, God knows, and we ..."

O'Gar scratched his head and turned away from Gatewood.

"In sight of Twin Peaks! There are hundreds of houses that are!"

Gatewood meanwhile had finished denouncing the telephone company and was pounding on his desk with a paperweight to attract our attention.

"Have you people done anything at all?" he demanded.

I answered him with another question: "Have you got the money ready?"

"No," he said, "I won't be held up by anybody!"

But he said it mechanically, without his usual conviction—the talk with his daughter had shaken him out of some of his stubbornness. He was thinking of her safety a little now instead of only his own fighting spirit.

We went at him hammer and tongs for a few minutes, and after a while he sent a clerk out for the money.

We split up the field then. Thode was to take some men from headquarters and see what he could find in the Twin Peaks end of

town; but we weren't very optimistic over the prospects there—
the territory was too large.

Lusk and O'Gar were to carefully mark the bills that the clerk
brought from the bank, and then stick as close to Gatewood as
they could without attracting attention. I was to go out to Gatewood's house and stay there.

The abductors had plainly instructed Gatewood to get the
money ready immediately so that they could arrange to get it on
short notice—not giving him time to communicate with anyone
or make plans.

Gatewood was to get hold of the newspapers, give them the
whole story, with the $10,000 reward he was offering for the ab-
ductors' capture, to be published as soon as the girl was safe—so
we would get the help of publicity at the earliest possible moment
without jeopardizing the girl.

The police in all the neighboring towns had already been notified—that had been done before the girl's phone message had
assured us that she was held in San Francisco.

Nothing happened at the Gatewood residence all that evening.
Harvey Gatewood came home early; and after dinner he paced
his library floor and drank whiskey until bedtime, demanding every few minutes that we, the detectives in the case, do something
besides sit around like a lot of damned mummies. O'Gar, Lusk,
and Thode were out in the street, keeping an eye on the house
and neighborhood.

At midnight Harvey Gatewood went to bed. I declined a bed in
favor of the library couch, which I dragged over beside the telephone, an extension of which was in Gatewood's bedroom.

At 2:30 the bell rang. I listened in while Gatewood talked from
his bed.

A man's voice, crisp and curt: "Gatewood?"

"Yes."

"Got the dough?"

"Yes."

Gatewood's voice was thick and blurred—I could imagine the boiling that was going on inside him.

"Good!" came the brisk voice. "Put a piece of paper around it and leave the house with it, right away! Walk down Clay Street, keeping on the same side as your house. Don't walk too fast and keep walking. If everything's all right, and there's no elbows tagging along, somebody'll come up to you between your house and the waterfront. They'll have a handkerchief up to their face for a second, and then they'll let it fall to the ground.

"When you see that, you'll lay the money on the pavement, turn around, and walk back to your house. If the money isn't marked, and you don't try any fancy tricks, you'll get your daughter back in an hour or two. If you try to pull anything—remember what we wrote you! Got it straight?"

Gatewood sputtered something that was meant for an affirmative, and the telephone clicked silent.

I didn't waste any of my precious time tracing the call—it would be from a public telephone, I knew—but yelled up the stairs to Gatewood:

"You do as you were told, and don't try any foolishness!"

Then I ran out into the early morning air to find the police detectives and the post-office inspector.

They had been joined by two plainclothesmen, and had two automobiles waiting. I told them what the situation was, and we laid hurried plans.

O'Gar was to drive in one of the cars down Sacramento Street, and Thode, in the other, down Washington Street. These streets parallel Clay, one on each side. They were to drive slowly, keeping pace with Gatewood, and stopping at each cross street to see that he passed.

When he failed to cross within a reasonable time they were to turn up to Clay Street—and their actions from then on would have to be guided by chance and their own wits.

Lusk was to wander along a block or two ahead of Gatewood, on the opposite side of the street, pretending to be mildly intoxicated.

I was to shadow Gatewood down the street, with one of the plainclothesmen behind me. The other plainclothesman was to turn in a call at headquarters for every available man to be sent to City Street. They would arrive too late, of course, and as likely as not it would take them some time to find us; but we had no way of knowing what was going to turn up before the night was over.

Our plan was sketchy enough, but it was the best we could do— we were afraid to grab whoever got the money from Gatewood. The girl's talk with her father that afternoon had sounded too much as if her captors were desperate for us to take any chances on going after them roughshod until she was out of their hands.

We had hardly finished our plans when Gatewood, wearing a heavy overcoat, left his house and turned down the street.

Farther down, Lusk, weaving along, talking to himself, was almost invisible in the shadows. There was no one else in sight. That meant that I had to give Gatewood at least two blocks' lead, so that the man who came for the money wouldn't tumble to me. One of the plainclothesmen was half a block behind me, on the other side of the street.

We walked two blocks down, and then a little chunky man in a derby hat came into sight. He passed Gatewood, passed me, went on.

Three blocks more.

A touring-car, large, black, powerfully engined, and with lowered curtains, came from the rear, passed us, went on. Possibly a scout. I scrawled its license number down on my pad without taking my hand out of my overcoat pocket.

Another three blocks.

A policeman passed, strolling along in ignorance of the game being played under his nose; and then a taxicab with a single male passenger. I wrote down its license number.

Four blocks with no one in sight ahead of me but Gatewood—I couldn't see Lusk any more.

Just ahead of Gatewood a man stepped out of a black doorway, turned around, called up to a window for someone to come down and open the door for him.

We went on.

Coming from nowhere, a woman stood on the sidewalk 50 feet ahead of Gatewood, a handkerchief to her face. It fluttered to the pavement.

Gatewood stopped, standing stifflegged. I could see his right hand come up, lifting the side of the overcoat in which it was pocketed—and I knew his hand was gripped around a pistol.

For perhaps half a minute he stood like a statue. Then his left hand came out of his pocket, and the bundle of money fell to the sidewalk in front of him, where it made a bright blur in the darkness. Gatewood turned abruptly, and began to retrace his steps homeward.

The woman had recovered her handkerchief. Now she ran to the bundle, picked it up, and scuttled to the black mouth of an alley a few feet distant—a rather tall woman, bent, and in dark clothes from head to feet.

In the black mouth of the alley she vanished.

I had been compelled to slow up while Gatewood and the woman stood facing each other, and I was more than a block away now. As soon as the woman disappeared, I took a chance and started pounding my rubber soles against the pavement.

The alley was empty when I reached it.

It ran all the way through to the next street, but I knew that the woman couldn't have reached the other end before I got to this one. I carry a lot of weight these days, but I can still step a block or two in good time. Along both sides of the alley were the rears of apartment buildings, each with its back door looking blankly, secretively, at me.

The plainclothesman who had been trailing behind me came up, then O'Gar and Thode in their cars, and soon, Lusk. O'Gar and Thode rode off immediately to wind through the neighboring streets, hunting for the woman. Lusk and the plainclothesman each planted himself on a corner from which two of the streets enclosing the block could be watched.

I went through the alley, hunting vainly for an unlocked door, an open window, a fire-escape that would show recent use—any of the signs that a hurried departure from the alley might leave.

Nothing!

O'Gar came back shortly with some reinforcements from headquarters that he had picked up, and Gatewood.

Gatewood was burning.

"Bungled the damn thing again! I won't pay your agency a nickel, and I'll see that some of these so-called detectives get put back in a uniform and set to walking beats!"

"What'd the woman look like?" I asked him.

"I don't know! I thought you were hanging around to take care of her! She was old and bent, kind of, I guess, but I couldn't see her face for her veil. I don't know! What the hell were you men doing? It's a damned outrage the way ..."

I finally got him quieted down and took him home, leaving the city men to keep the neighborhood under surveillance. There were fourteen or fifteen of them on the job now, and every shadow held at least one.

The girl would head for home as soon as she was released and I wanted to be there to pump her. There was an excellent chance of catching her abductors before they got very far, if she could tell us anything at all about them.

Home, Gatewood went up against the whiskey bottle again, while I kept one ear cocked at the telephone and the other at the front door. O'Gar or Thode phoned every half hour or so to ask if we'd heard from the girl.

They had still found nothing.

At 9 o'clock they, with Lusk, arrived at the house. The woman in black had turned out to be a man, and had got away.

In the rear of one of the apartment buildings that touched the alley—just a foot or so within the back-door—they found a wom-

an's skirt, long coat, hat and veil—all black. Investigating the occupants of the house, they had learned that an apartment had been
rented to a young man named Leighton three days before.

Leighton was not at home, when they went up to his apartment.
His rooms held a lot of cold cigarette butts, an empty bottle, and
nothing else that had not been there when he rented it.

The inference was clear: he had rented the apartment so that he
might have access to the building. Wearing women's clothes over
his own, he had gone out of the back door—leaving it unlatched
behind him—to meet Gatewood. Then he had run back into the
building, discarded his disguise, and hurried through the building,
out the front door, and away before we had our feeble net around
the block—perhaps dodging into dark doorways here and there
to avoid O'Gar and Thode in their cars.

Leighton, it seemed, was a man of about 30, slender, about five
feet eight or nine inches tall, with dark hair and eyes; rather good-
looking, and well-dressed on the two occasions when people living
in the building had seen him, in a brown suit and a light brown
felt hat.

There was no possibility, according to both of the detectives
and the post-office inspector, that the girl might have been held,
even temporarily, in Leighton's apartment.

Ten o'clock came, and no word from the girl.

Gatewood had lost his domineering bullheadedness by now
and was breaking up. The suspense was getting him, and the liquor he had put away wasn't helping him. I didn't like him either
personally or by reputation, but this morning I felt sorry for him.

I talked to the Agency over the phone and got the reports of
the operatives who had been looking up Audrey's friends. The last
person to see her had been an Agnes Dangerfield, who had seen
her walking down Market Street near Sixth, alone, on the night
of her abduction—some time between 8:15 and 8:45. Audrey had
been too far away for the Dangerfield girl to speak to her.

For the rest, the boys had learned nothing except that Audrey was a wild, spoiled youngster who hadn't shown any great care in selecting her friends—just the sort of girl who could easily fall into the hands of a mob of highbinders*.

Noon struck. No sign of the girl. We told the newspapers to turn loose the story, with the added developments of the past few hours.

Gatewood was broken; he sat with his head in his hands, looking at nothing. Just before I left to follow a hunch I had, he looked up at me, and I'd never have recognized him if I hadn't seen the change take place.

"What do you think is keeping her away?" he asked.

I didn't have the heart to tell him what I had every reason to suspect, now that the money had been paid and she had failed to show up. So I stalled with some vague assurances, and left.

I caught a cab and dropped off in the shopping district. I visited the five largest department stores, going to all the women's wear departments from shoes to hats, and trying to learn if a man—perhaps one answering Leighton's description—had been buying clothes in the past couple days that would fit Audrey Gatewood.

Failing to get any results, I turned the rest of the local stores over to one of the boys from the Agency, and went across the bay to canvass the Oakland stores.

At the first one I got action. A man who might easily have been Leighton had been in the day before, buying clothes of Audrey's size. He had bought lots of them, everything from lingerie to a coat, and—my luck was hitting on all cylinders—had had his purchases delivered to T. Offord, at an address on Fourteenth Street.

At the Fourteenth Street address, an apartment house, I found Mr. and Mrs. Theodore Offord's names in the vestibule for Apartment 202.

I had just found the apartment number when the front door opened and a stout, middle-aged woman in a gingham house-dress came out. She looked at me a bit curiously, so I asked:

---

* Chinese thugs

"Do you know where I can find the superintendent?"

"I'm the superintendent," she said.

I handed her a card and stepped indoors with her.

"I'm from the bonding department of the North American Casualty Company"—a repetition of the lie that was printed on the card I had given her—"and a bond for Mr. Offord has been applied for. Is he all right so far as you know?" With the slightly apologetic air of one going through with a necessary but not too important formality.

"A bond? That's funny! He is going away tomorrow."

"Well, I can't say what the bond is for," I said lightly. "We investigators just get the names and addresses. It may be for his present employer, or perhaps the man he is going to work for has applied for it. Or some firms have us look up prospective employees before they hire them, just to be safe."

"Mr. Offord, so far as I know, is a very nice young man," she said, "but he has been here only a week."

"Not staying long, then?"

"No. They came here from Denver, intending to stay, but the low altitude doesn't agree with Mrs. Offord, so they are going back."

"Are you sure they came from Denver?"

"Well," she said, "they told me they did."

"How many of them are there?"

"Only the two of them; they're young people."

"Well, how do they impress you?" I asked, trying to get over the impression that I thought her a woman of shrewd judgment.

"They seem to be a very nice young couple. You'd hardly know they were in their apartment most of the time, they're so quiet. I'm sorry they can't stay."

"Do they go out much?"

"I really don't know. They have their keys, and unless I should happen to pass them going in or out I'd never see them."

"Then, as a matter of fact you couldn't say whether they stayed away all night some nights or not. Could you?"

She eyed me doubtfully—I was stepping way over my pretext

now, but I didn't think it mattered—and shook her head.

"No, I couldn't say."

"They have many visitors?"

"I don't know. Mr. Offord is not—"

She broke off as a man came in quietly from the street, brushed past me, and started to mount the steps to the second floor.

"Oh, dear!" she whispered. "I hope he didn't hear me talking about him. That's Mr. Offord."

A slender man in brown, with a light brown hat—Leighton perhaps.

I hadn't seen anything of him except his back, nor he anything except mine. I watched him as he climbed the stairs. If he had heard the woman mention his name he would use the turn at the head of the stairs to sneak a look at me.

He did.

I kept my face stolid, but I knew him.

He was "Penny" Quayle, a con man who had been active in the East four or five years before.

His face was as expressionless as mine. But he knew me.

A door on the second floor shut. I left the woman and started for the stairs.

"I think I'll go up and talk to him," I told her.

Coming silently to the door of Apartment 202, I listened. Not a sound. This was no time for hesitation. I pressed the bell-button.

As close together as the tapping of three keys under the fingers of an expert typist, but a thousand times more vicious, came three pistol shots. And waist-high in the door of Apartment 202 were three bullet holes.

The three bullets would have been in my fat carcass if I hadn't learned years ago to stand to one side of strange doors when making uninvited calls.

Inside the apartment sounded a man's voice, sharp, commanding.

"Cut it, kid! For God's sake, not that!"

A woman's voice, shrill, bitter, spiteful, screaming blasphemies.

Two more bullets came through the door.

"Stop! No! No!" The man's voice had a note of fear in it now.

The woman's voice, cursing hotly. A scuffle. A shot that didn't hit the door.

I hurled my foot against the door, near the knob, and the lock broke away.

On the floor of the room, a man—Quayle—and a woman were tussling. He was bending over her, holding her wrists, trying to keep her down. A smoking pistol was in one of her hands. I got to it in a jump and tore it loose.

"That's enough!" I called to them when I was planted. "Get up and receive company."

Quayle released his antagonist's wrists, whereupon she shuck at his eyes with curved, sharp-nailed fingers, tearing his cheek open. He scrambled away from her on hands and knees, and both of them got to their feet.

He sat down on a chair immediately, panting and wiping his bleeding cheek with a handkerchief.

She stood, hands on hips, in the center of the room, glaring at me.

"I suppose," she spat, "you think you've raised hell!"

I laughed—I could afford to.

"If your father is in his right mind," I told her, "he'll do it with a razor strap when he gets you home again. A fine joke you picked out to play on him!"

"If *you'd* been tied to him as long as I have, and had been bullied and held down as much, I guess *you'd* do most anything to get enough money so that you could go away and live your own life."

I didn't say anything to that. Remembering some of the business methods Harvey Gatewood had used—particularly some of his war contracts that the Department of Justice was still investigating—I suppose the worst that could be said about Audrey was that she was her father's own daughter.

"How'd you rap to it?" Quayle asked me, politely.

"Several ways," I said. "First, one of Audrey's friends saw her on

Market Street between 8:15 and 8:45 the night she disappeared; and your letter to Gatewood was postmarked 9 P.M. Pretty fast work. You should have waited a while before mailing it. I suppose she dropped it in the post office on her way over here?"

Quayle nodded.

"Then second," I went on, "there was that phone call of hers. She knew it took anywhere from ten to fifteen minutes to get her father on the wire at the office. If she had gotten to a phone while imprisoned, time would have been so valuable that she'd have told her story to the first person she got hold of—the switchboard operator, most likely. So that made it look as if, besides wanting to throw out that Twin Peaks line, she wanted to stir the old man out of his bullheadedness.

"When she failed to show up after the money was paid, I figured it was a sure bet that she had kidnaped herself. I knew that if she came back home after faking this thing, we'd find it out before we'd talked to her very long—and I figured she knew that too, and would stay away.

"The rest was easy—I got some good breaks. We knew a man was working with her after we found the woman's clothes you left behind, and I took a chance on there being no one else in it. Then I figured she'd need clothes—she couldn't have taken any from home without tipping her mitt—and there was an even chance that she hadn't laid in a stock beforehand. She's got too many girl friends of the sort that do a lot of shopping to make it safe for her to have risked showing herself in stores. Maybe, then, the man would buy what she needed. And it turned out that he did, and that he was too lazy to carry away his purchases, or perhaps there was too many of them, and so he had them sent out. That's the story."

Quayle nodded again.

"I was damned careless," he said, and then, jerking a contemptuous thumb toward the girl. "But what can you expect? She's had a skinful of hop ever since we started. Took all my time and attention keeping her from running wild and gumming the works. Just now was a sample—I told her you were coming up and she goes crazy and tries to add your corpse to the wreckage!"

The Gatewood reunion took place in the office of the captain of inspectors, on the second floor of the Oakland City Hall, and it was a merry little party.

For over an hour it was a toss-up whether Harvey Gatewood would die of apoplexy, strangle his daughter, or send her off to the state reformatory until she was of age. But Audrey licked him. Besides being a chip off the old block, she was young enough to be careless of consequences, while her father, for all his bullhead-edness, had had some caution hammered into him.

The card she beat him with was a threat of spilling everything she knew about him to the newspapers, and at least one of the San Francisco papers had been trying to get his scalp for years.

I don't know what she had on him, and I don't think he was any too sure himself; but, with his war contracts still being investi-gated by the Department of Justice, he couldn't afford to take a chance. There was no doubt at all that she would have done as she threatened.

And so, together, they left for home, sweating hate for each other from every pore.

We took Quayle upstairs and put him in a cell, but he was too experienced to let that worry him. He knew that if the girl was to be spared, he himself couldn't very easily be convicted of anything.

I was glad it was over. It had been a tough caper.

SLIPPERY FINGERS

"YOU ARE already familiar, of course, with the particulars of my father's—ah—death?"

"The papers are full of it, and have been for three days," I said, "and I've read them; but I'll have to have the story firsthand."

"There isn't very much to tell."

This Frederick Grover was a short, slender man of something under thirty years, and dressed like a picture out of *Vanity Fair.*[*] His almost girlish features and voice did nothing to make him more impressive, but I began to forget these things after a few minutes. He wasn't a sap. I knew that downtown, where he was rapidly building up a large and lively business in stocks and bonds without calling for too much help from his father's millions, he was considered a shrewd article; and I wasn't surprised later when Benny Forman, who ought to know, told me that Frederick Grover was the best poker player west of Chicago.

"Father has lived here alone with the servants since mother's death, two years ago," he went on. "I am married, you know, and live in town. Last Saturday evening he dismissed Barton—Barton was his butler-valet, and had been with father for quite a few years—at a little after nine, saying that he did not want to be disturbed during the evening.

"Father was here in the library at the time, looking through

---

[*] American style magazine, founded in 1913, focusing on fashion and popular culture

some papers. The servants' rooms are in the rear, and none of the servants seem to have heard anything during the night.

"At seven-thirty the following morning—Sunday—Barton found father lying on the floor, just to the right of where you are sitting, dead, stabbed in the throat with the brass paper knife that was always kept on the table here. The front door was ajar.

"The police found bloody fingerprints on the knife, the table, and the front door; but so far they have not found the man who left the prints, which is why I am employing your agency. The physician who came with the police placed the time of father's death at between eleven o'clock and midnight.

"Later, on Monday, we learned that father had drawn ten thousand dollars in hundred-dollar bills from the bank Saturday morning. No trace of the money has been found. My fingerprints, as well as the servants', were compared with the ones found by the police, but there was no similarity. I think that is all."

"Do you know of any enemies your father had ?"

"I know of none, though he may have had them. You see, I really didn't know my father very well. He was a very reticent man and, until his retirement, about five years ago, he spent most of his time in South America, where most of his mining interests were. He may have had dozens of enemies, though Barton—who probably knew more about him than anyone—seems to know of no one who hated father enough to kill him."

"How about relatives?"

"I was his heir and only child, if that is what you are getting at. So far as I know he had no other living relatives."

"I'll talk to the servants," I said.

The maid and the cook could tell me nothing, and I learned very little more from Barton. He had been with Henry Grover since nineteen twelve, had been with him in Yunnan, Peru, Mexico, and Central America, but apparently he knew little or nothing of his master's business or acquaintances.

He said that Grover had not seemed excited or worried on

the night of the murder, and that nearly every night Grover dismissed him at about the same time, with orders that he not be disturbed; so no importance was to be attached to that part of it. He knew of no one with whom Grover had communicated during the day, and he had not seen the money Grover had drawn from the bank.

I made a quick inspection of the house and grounds, not expecting to find anything; and I didn't. Half the jobs that come to a private detective are like this one: three or four days—and often as many weeks—have passed since the crime was committed. The police work on the job until they are stumped; then the injured party calls in a private sleuth, dumps him down on a trail that is old and cold and badly trampled, and expects—Oh, well! I picked out this way of making a living, so . . .

I looked through Grover's papers—he had a safe and a desk full of them—but didn't find anything to get excited about. They were mostly columns of figures.

"I'm going to send an accountant out here to go over your father's books," I told Frederick Grover. "Give him everything he asks for, and fix it up with the bank so they'll help him."

I caught a streetcar and went back to town, called at Ned Root's office, and headed him out toward Grover's. Ned is a human adding machine with educated eyes, ears, and nose. He can spot a kink in a set of books farther than I can see the covers.

"Keep digging until you find something, Ned, and you can charge Grover whatever you like. Give me something to work on—quick!"

The murder had all the earmarks of one that had grown out of blackmail, though there was—there always is—a chance that it might have been something else. But it didn't look like the work of an enemy or a burglar: either of them would have packed his weapon with him, would not have trusted to finding it on the grounds. Of course, if Frederick Grover, or one of the servants, had killed Henry Grover . . . but the fingerprints said "No."

Just to play safe, I put in a few hours getting a line on Frederick. He had been at a ball on the night of the murder; he had never, so far as I could learn, quarreled with his father; his father was liberal with him, giving him everything he wanted; and Frederick was taking in more money in his brokerage office than he was spending. No motive for a murder appeared on the surface there.

At the city detective bureau I hunted up the police sleuths who had been assigned to the murder, Marty O'Hara and George Dean. It didn't take them long to tell me what they knew about it. Whoever had made the bloody fingerprints was not known to the police here: they had not found the prints in their files. The classifications had been broadcast to every large city in the country, but with no results so far.

A house four blocks from Grover's had been robbed on the night of the murder, and there was a slim chance that the same man *might* have been responsible for both jobs. But the burglary had occurred after one o'clock in the morning, which made the connection look not so good. A burglar who had killed a man, and perhaps picked up ten thousand dollars in the bargain, wouldn't be likely to turn his hand to another job right away.

I looked at the paper knife with which Grover had been killed, and at the photographs of the bloody prints, but they couldn't help me much just now. There seemed to be nothing to do but get out and dig around until I turned up something somewhere.

Then the door opened, and Joseph Clane was ushered into the room where O'Hara, Dean and I were talking.

Clane was a hard-bitten citizen, for all his prosperous look; fifty or fifty-five, I'd say, with eyes, mouth and jaw that held plenty of humor but none of what is sometimes called the milk of human kindness.

He was a big man, beefy, and all dressed up in a tight-fitting checkered suit, fawn-colored hat, patent-leather shoes with buff uppers, and the rest of the things that go with that sort of combination. He had a harsh voice that was as empty of expression as his hard red face, and he held his body stiffly, as if he were afraid that the buttons on his too tight clothes were about to pop off. Even his arms hung woodenly at his sides, with thick fingers that were lifelessly motionless.

He came right to the point. He had been a friend of the murdered man's, and thought that perhaps what he could tell us would be of value.

He had met Henry Grover—he called him "Henny"—in eighteen ninety-four, in Ontario, where Grover was working a claim, the gold mine that had started the murdered man along the road to wealth. Clane had been employed by Grover as foreman, and the two men had become close friends. A man named Denis Waldeman had a claim adjoining Grover's and a dispute had arisen over their boundaries. The dispute ran on for some time—the men coming to blows once or twice—but finally Grover seems to have triumphed, for Waldeman suddenly left the country.

Clane's idea was that if we could find Waldeman we might find Grover's murderer, for Waldeman was "a mean cuss, for a fact," and not likely to have forgotten his defeat.

Clane and Grover had kept in touch with each other, corresponding or meeting at irregular intervals, but the murdered man had never said or written anything that would throw light on his death. Clane, too, had given up mining, and now had a small string of race horses which occupied all his time.

He was in the city for a rest between racing-meets, had arrived two days before the murder, but had been too busy with his own affairs—he had discharged his trainer and was trying to find another—to call upon his friend. Clane was staying at the Marquis Hotel, and would be in the city for a week longer.

"How come you've waited three days before coming to tell us all this?" Dean asked him.

"I wasn't noways sure I had ought to do it. I wasn't never sure in my mind but what maybe Henny done for that fellow Waldeman—he disappeared sudden-like. And I didn't want to do nothing to dirty Henny's name. But finally I decided to do the right thing. And then there's another thing: you found some fingerprints in Henny's house, didn't you? The newspapers said so."

"We did."

"Well, I want you to take mine and match them up. I was out with a girl the night of the murder"—he leered suddenly, boastingly—"all night! And she's a good girl, got a husband and a lot of folks; and it wouldn't be right to drag her into this to prove that I wasn't in Henny's house when he was killed, in case you'd maybe think I killed him. So I thought I better come down here, tell you all about it, and get you to take my fingerprints, and have it all over with."

We went up to the identification bureau and had Clane's prints taken. They were not at all like the murderer's.

After we pumped Clane dry I went out and sent a telegram to our Toronto office, asking them to get a line on the Waldeman angle. Then I hunted up a couple of boys who eat, sleep, and breathe horse racing. They told me that Clane was well known in racing circles as the owner of a small string of near-horses* that ran as irregularly as the stewards would permit.

At the Marquis Hotel I got hold of the house detective, who is a helpful chap so long as his hand is kept greased.† He verified my information about Clane's status in the sporting world, and told me that Clane had stayed at the hotel for several days at a time, off and on, within the past couple years.

He tried to trace Clane's telephone calls for me but—as usual when you want them—the records were jumbled. I arranged to have the girls on the switchboard listen in on any talking he did during the next few days.

Ned Root was waiting for me when I got down to the office the next morning. He had worked on Grover's accounts all night, and

---

*   plow horses
†   paid off

had found enough to give me a start. Within the past year—that was as far back as Ned had gone—Grover had drawn out of his bank accounts nearly fifty thousand dollars that couldn't be accounted for; nearly fifty thousand exclusive of the ten thousand he had drawn the day of the murder. Ned gave me the amounts and the dates:

May 6, 1922	*$15,000*
June 10, 1922	*$5,000*
August 1, 1922	*$5,000*
October 10, 1922	*$10,000*
January 3, 1923	*$12,500*

Forty-seven thousand, five hundred dollars! Somebody was getting fat off him! The local managers of the telegraph companies raised the usual howl about respecting their patrons' privacy, but I got an order from the Prosecuting Attorney and put a clerk at work on the files of each office.

Then I came back to the Marquis Hotel and looked at the old registers. Clane had been there from May 4th to 7th, and from October 8th to 15th last year. That checked off two of the dates upon which Grover had made his withdrawals.

I had to wait until nearly six o'clock for my information from the telegraph companies, but it was worth waiting for. On the third of last January Henry Grover had telegraphed twelve thousand, five hundred dollars to Joseph Clane in San Diego. The clerks hadn't found anything on the other dates I had given them, but I wasn't at all dissatisfied. I had Joseph Clane fixed as the man who had been getting fat off Grover.

I sent Dick Foley—he is the Agency's shadow ace—and Bob Teal—a youngster who will be a world-beater some day—over to Clane's hotel.

"Plant yourselves in the lobby," I told them. "I'll be over in a few minutes to talk to Clane, and I'll try to bring him down in the lobby where you can get a good look at him. Then I want him shadowed until he shows up at police headquarters tomorrow. I want to know where he goes and who he talks to. And if he spends much time talking to any one person, or their conversation seems very important, I want one of you boys to trail the other man, to see who he is and what he does. If Clane tries to blow town, grab him and have him thrown in the can."

I gave Dick and Bob time enough to get themselves placed, and then went to the hotel. Clane was out, so I waited. He came in a little after eleven and I went up to his room with him. I didn't hem-and-haw, but came out cold-turkey:

"All the signs point to Grover's having been blackmailed. Do you know anything about it?"

"No," he said.

"Grover drew a lot of money out of his banks at different times. You got some of it, I know, and I suppose you got most of it. What about it?"

He didn't pretend to be insulted, or even surprised by my talk. He smiled a little grimly, maybe, but as if he thought it the most natural thing in the world for me to suspect him.

"I told you that me and Henny were pretty chummy, didn't I? Well, you ought to know that all us fellows that fool with the bang-tails* have our streaks of bad luck. Whenever I'd get up against it I'd hit Henny up for a stake; like at Tijuana last winter where I got into a flock of bad breaks. Henny lent me twelve or fifteen thousand and I got back on my feet again. I've done that often. He ought to have some of my letters and wires in his stuff. If you look through his things you'll find them."

I didn't pretend that I believed him.

"Suppose you drop into police headquarters at nine in the morning and we'll go over everything with the city dicks," I told him.

And then, to make my play stronger:

---

* horses

"I wouldn't make it much later than nine—they might be out looking for you."

"Uh-huh," was all the answer I got.

I went back to the Agency and planted myself within reach of a telephone, waiting for word from Dick and Bob. I thought I was sitting pretty. Clane had been blackmailing Grover—I didn't have a single doubt of that—and I didn't think he had been very far away when Grover was killed. That woman alibi of his sounded all wrong!

But the bloody fingerprints were not Clane's—unless the police identification bureau had pulled an awful boner—and the man who had left the prints was the bird I was setting my cap for. Clane had let three days pass between the murder and his appearance at headquarters. The natural explanation for that would be that his partner, the actual murderer, had needed nearly that much time to put himself in the clear.

My present game was simple: I had stirred Clane up with the knowledge that he was still suspected, hoping that he would have to repeat whatever precautions were necessary to protect his accomplice in the first place.

He had taken three days then. I was giving him about nine hours now: time enough to do something, but not too much time, hoping that he would have to hurry things along and that in his haste he would give Dick and Bob a chance to turn up his partner.

At a quarter to one in the morning Dick telephoned that Clane had left the hotel a few minutes behind me, had gone to an apartment house on Polk Street, and was still there.

I went up to Polk Street and joined Dick and Bob. They told me that Clane had gone in apartment number twenty-seven, and that the directory in the vestibule showed that this apartment was occupied by George Farr. I stuck around with the boys until two o'clock, when I went home for some sleep.

At seven I was with them again, and was told that our man had not appeared yet. It was a little after eight when he came out and turned down Geary Street, with the boys trailing him, while I went into the apartment house for a talk with the manager. She told me that Farr had been living there for four or five months, lived alone, and was a photographer by trade.

I went up and rang his bell. He was a husky of thirty or thirty-two with bleary eyes that looked as if they hadn't had much sleep that night. I didn't waste any time with him.

"I'm from the Continental Detective Agency and I am interested in Joseph Clane. What do you know about him?"

He was wide awake now.

"Nothing."

"Do you know him?"

"No."

"Farr," I said, "I want you to go down to headquarters with me.

He moved like a streak and his sullen manner had me a little off my guard; but I turned my head in time to take the punch above my ear instead of on the chin. At that, it carried me off my feet and I wouldn't have bet a nickel that my skull wasn't dented; but luck was with me and I fell across the doorway, holding the door open, and managed to scramble up, stumble through some rooms and catch one of his feet as it was going through the bathroom window to join its mate on the fire escape. I got a split lip in the scuffle, but he behaved after a while.

I didn't stop to look at his stuff—that could be done more regularly later—but put him in a taxicab and took him to the Hall of Justice. I was afraid that if I waited too long Clane would take a run-out on me.

Clane's mouth fell open when he saw Farr, but neither of them said anything.

I was feeling pretty chirp* in spite of my bruises.

"Let's get this bird's fingerprints and get it over with," I said to O'Hara.

Dean was not in.

---

* chipper

"And keep an eye on Clane. I think maybe he'll have another story to tell us in a few minutes."

We got in the elevator and took our men up to the identification bureau, where we put Farr's fingers on the pad. Phels—he is the department's expert—took one look at the results and turned to me.

"Well, what of it?"

"What of what?" I asked.

"This isn't the man who killed Henry Grover!"

Clane laughed, Farr laughed, O'Hara laughed and Phels laughed. I didn't! I stood there and pretended to be thinking, trying to get myself in hand.

"Are you sure you haven't made a mistake?" I blurted.

You can tell how badly upset I was by that: it's plain suicide to say a thing like that to a fingerprint expert!

Phels didn't answer; just looked me up and down.

Clane laughed again, and turned his ugly face to me.

"Do you want to take my prints again, Mr. Detective?"

"Yeah," I said, "just that!"

I had to say something.

Clane held his hands out to Phels, who ignored them, speaking to me with heavy sarcasm.

"Better take them yourself this time, so you'll be sure it's been done right."

I was mad clean through—of course it was my own fault—but I was pig-headed enough to go through with anything, particularly anything that would hurt somebody's feelings, so I said:

"That's not a bad idea!"

I walked over and took hold of one of Clane's hands. I'd never taken a fingerprint before, but I had seen it done often enough to throw a bluff. I started to ink Clane's fingers and found that I was holding them wrong—my own fingers were in the way.

Then I came back to earth. The balls of Clane's fingers were too smooth—or rather, too slick—without the slight clinging feeling that belongs to flesh. I turned his hand over so fast that I nearly upset him and looked at the fingers. I didn't know what I had expected to find but I didn't find anything—not anything that I could name.

"Phels," I called, "look here!"

He forgot his injured feelings and bent to look at Clane's hand.

"I'll be——" he began, and then the two of us were busy for a few minutes taking Clane down and sitting on him, while O'Hara quieted Farr, who had also gone suddenly into action.

When things were peaceful again Phels examined Clane's hands carefully, scratching the fingers with a fingernail.

He jumped up, leaving me to hold Clane, and paying no attention to my, "What is it?" got a cloth and some liquid, and washed the fingers thoroughly. We took his prints again. They matched the bloody ones taken from Grover's house!

Then we all sat down and had a nice talk.

"I told you about the trouble Henny had with that fellow Waldeman," Clane began, after he and Farr had decided to come clean: there was nothing else they could do. "And how he won out in the argument because Waldeman disappeared. Well, Henny done for* him—shot him one night and buried him—and I saw it. Grover was one bad actor in them days, a tough *hombre* to tangle with, so I didn't try to make nothing out of what I knew.

"But after he got older and richer he got soft—a lot of men go like that—and must have begun worrying over it; because when I ran into him in New York accidentally about four years ago it didn't take me long to learn that he was pretty well tamed, and he told me that he hadn't been able to forget the look on Waldeman's face when he drilled him.

"So I took a chance and braced Henny for a couple thousand. I got them easy, and after that, whenever I was flat I either went to him or sent him word, and he always came across. But I was careful not to crowd him too far. I knew what a terror he was in the old days, and I didn't want to push him into busting loose.

---

*   killed

"But that's what I did in the end. I phoned him Friday that I needed money and he said he'd call me up and let me know where to meet him the next night. He called up around half past nine Saturday night and told me to come out to the house. So I went out there and he was waiting for me on the porch and took me upstairs and gave me the ten thousand.

"Naturally I wanted to get away as soon as I had the money but he must have felt sort of talkative for a change, because he kept me there for half an hour or so, gassing about men we used to know up in the province.

"After a while I began to get nervous. He was getting a look in his eyes like he used to have when he was young. And then all of a sudden he flared up and tied into me. He had me by the throat and was bending me back across the table when my hand touched that brass knife. It was either me or him—so I let him have it where it would do the most good.

"I beat it then and went back to the hotel. The newspapers were full of it next day, and had a whole lot of stuff about bloody fingerprints. That gave me a jolt! I didn't know nothing about fingerprints, and here I'd left them all over the dump.

"And then I got to worrying over the whole thing, and it seemed like Henny must have my name written down somewheres among his papers, and maybe had saved some of my letters or telegrams. I figured the police would want to be asking me some questions sooner or later; and there I'd be with fingers that fit the bloody prints, and nothing for what Farr calls a alibi.

"That's when I thought of Farr. I had his address and I knew he had been a fingerprint sharp in the East, so I decided to take a chance on him. I went to him and told him the whole story and between us we figured out what to do.

"He said he'd dope my fingers, and I was to come here and tell the story we'd fixed up, and have my fingerprints taken, and then I'd be safe no matter what leaked out about me and Henny. So he smeared up the fingers and told me to be careful not to shake hands with anybody or touch anything, and I came down here and everything went like three of a kind.

"Then that little fat guy"—meaning me—"came around to the hotel last night and as good as told me that he thought I had done for Henny and that I better come down here this morning. I beat it for Farr's right away to see whether I ought to run for it or sit tight, and Farr said, 'Sit tight!' So I stayed there all night and he fixed up my hands this morning."

Phels turned to Farr.

"I've seen faked prints before, but never any this good. How'd you do it?"

These scientific birds are funny. Here was Farr looking a nice, long stretch in the face as "accessory after the fact," and yet he brightened up under the admiration in Phels's tone and answered with a voice that was chock-full of pride.

"It's simple! I got hold of a man whose prints I knew weren't in any police gallery—I didn't want any slip-up there—and took his prints and put them on a copper plate, using the ordinary photoengraving process, but etching it pretty deep. Then I coated Clane's fingers with gelatin—just enough to cover all his markings—and pressed them against the plates. That way I got everything, even to the pores, and . . ."

When I left the bureau ten minutes later Farr and Phels were still sitting knee to knee, jabbering away at each other as only a couple of birds who are cuckoo on the same subject can.

THE GREEN ELEPHANT

JOE SHUPE stood in the doorway of the square-faced office build-ing—his body tilted slantwise so that one thin shoulder, lodged against the gray stone, helped his crossed legs hold him up—look-ing without interest into the street.

He had stepped into the vestibule to roll a cigarette out of reach of the boisterous wind that romped along Riverside Avenue, and he had remained there because he had nothing better to do. In fact, he had nothing else to do just now. Tomorrow he would revisit the employment offices—a matter of a few blocks' walk along Main and Trent Avenues, with brief digressions into one or two of the inter-secting streets—for the fifth consecutive day; perhaps to be reward-ed by a job, perhaps to hear reiterations of the now familiar "noth-ing in your line today." But the time for that next pilgrimage was still some twenty hours away; so Joe Shupe loitered in the doorway, and dull thoughts began to crawl around in his little round head.

He thought of the Swede first, with distaste. The Swede—he was a Dane, but the distinction was too subtle for Joe—had come down to the city from a Lost Creek lumber camp with money in his pockets and faith in his fellows. When the men came together and formed their brief friendship only fifty dollars remained of the Swede's tangible wealth. Joe got that by a crude and hoary subterfuge with which even a timber-beast from Lost Creek should have been familiar. What became of the swindled Swede's faith is not a matter of record. Joe had not given *that* a thought.

But what was vital to Joe Shupe was that, inspired by the ease with which he had gained the fifty dollars, he had deserted the polished counter over which for eight hours each day he had shoved pies and sandwiches and coffee, and had set out to live by his wits. But the fifty dollars had soon dribbled away, the Swede had had no successors; and now Joe Shupe was beset with the necessity of finding employment again.

Joe's fault, as Doc Haire had once pointed out, was that he was an unskilled laborer in the world of crime, and therefore had to content himself with stealing whatever came to hand—a slipshod and generally unsatisfactory method. As the same authority had often declared: "Making a living on the mace ain't duck soup! Take half these guys you hear telling the world what wonders they are at puffing boxes, knocking over joints, and the rest of the lays—not a half of 'em makes three meals a day at it! Then what chance has a guy that ain't got no regular racket, but's got to trust to luck, got? Huh?"

But Joe Shupe had disregarded this advice, and even the oracle's own example. For Doc Haire, although priding himself upon being the most altogether efficient house-burglar in the Northwest, was not above shipping out into the Coeur d'Alenes now and then to repair his finances by a few weeks' work in the mines. Joe realized that Doc had been right; that he himself was not equipped to dig through the protecting surfaces with which mankind armored its wealth; that the Swede's advent had been a fortuitous episode, and a recurrence could not be expected. He blamed the Swede now.

A commotion in the street interrupted Joe Shupe's introspection.

Across the street two automobiles were twisting and turning, backing and halting, in clumsy dance figures. Men began to run back and forth between them. A tall man in a black overcoat stood up in one of the cars and began shooting with a small-caliber pistol at indeterminate targets. Weapons appeared in the other automobiles, and in the hands of men in the street between the two machines. Spectators scrambled into doorways. From down the street a policeman was running heavily, tugging at his hip, and trying to free his wrist from an entangling coattail. A man was running across the street toward Joe's doorway, a black Gladstone bag swinging at his side. As the man's foot touched the curb he fell forward, sprawling half in the gutter, half on the sidewalk. The bag left his hand and slid across the pavement—balancing itself as nicely as a boy on skates—to Joe's feet.

The wisdom of Doc Haire went for nothing. With no thought for the economics of thievery, the amenities of specialization, Joe Shupe followed his bent. He picked up the bag, passed through the revolving door into the lobby of the building, turned a corner, followed a corridor, and at length came to a smaller door, through which he reached an alley. The alley gave to another street and a streetcar that had paused to avoid a truck. Joe climbed into the car.

Thus far Joe Shupe had been guided by pure instinct, and—granting that to touch the bag at all were judicious—had acted deftly and with beautiful precision. But now his conscious brain caught up with him as it were, and resumed its dominion over him. He began to wonder what he had let himself in for, whether his prize were worth the risk its possession had entailed; just how great that risk might be. He became excited, his pulse throbbed, singing in his temples, and his mouth went dry. He had a vision of innumerable policemen, packed in taxicabs like pullets in crates, racing dizzily to intercept him.

He got to the street four blocks from where he had boarded the streetcar, and only a suspicion that the conductor was watching him persuaded him to cling to the bag. He would have preferred leaving it inconspicuously between the seats, to be found in the carbarn. He walked rapidly away from the car line, turning thankfully each corner the city put in his path, until he came to another row of car tracks. He stayed on the second car for six blocks, and then wound circuitously through the streets again, finally coming to the hotel in which he had his room.

A towel covering the keyhole, the blind down over the one

narrow window, Joe Shupe put the bag on his bed and set about opening it. It was securely locked, but with his knife he attacked a leather side, making a ragged slit through which he looked into depths of green paper.

"Holy hell!" his gaping mouth exclaimed. "All the money in the world!"

He straightened abruptly, listening, while his small brown eyes looked suspiciously around the room. Tiptoeing to the door, he listened again; unlocked the door quickly and flung it open; searched the dark hall. Then he returned to the black bag. Enlarging the opening, he dumped and raked his spoils out on the bed: a mound of gray-green paper—a bushel of it—neatly divided into little soft, paper-gartered bricks. Thousands, hundreds, tens, twenties, fifties! For a long minute he stood open-mouthed, spellbound, panting; then he hastily covered the pile of currency with one of the shabby gray blankets on the bed, and dropped weakly down beside it.

Presently the desire to know the amount of his loot penetrated Joe's stupefaction and he set about counting the money. He counted slowly and with difficulty, taking one package of bills out of its hiding place at a time and stowing it under another blanket when be had finished with it. He counted each package he handled, bill by bill, ignoring the figures printed on the Manila wrappers. At fifty thousand he stopped, estimating that he had handled one-third of the pile. The emotional seething within him, together with the effort the unaccustomed addition required of his brain, had by then driven his curiosity away.

His mind, freed of its mathematical burden, was attacked by an alarming thought. The manager of the hotel, who was his own clerk, had seen Joe come in with the bag; and while the bag was not unusual in appearance, nevertheless, any black bag would attract both eyes and speculation after the evening papers were read. Joe decided that he would have to get out of the hotel, after which the bag would have to be disposed of.

Laboriously, and at the cost of two large blisters, he hacked at the bag with his dull knife and bent it until, wrapped in an old newspaper, it made a small and unassuming bundle. Then he distributed the money about his person, stuffing his pockets and even putting some of the bills inside his shirt. He looked at his reflection in the mirror when he had finished, and the result was very unsatisfactory: he presented a decidedly padded appearance.

That would not do. He dragged his battered valise from under the bed and put the money into it, under his few clothes.

There was no delay about his departure from the hotel: it was of the type where all bills are payable in advance. He passed four rubbish cans before he could summon the courage to get rid of the fragments of the bag, but he boldly dropped them into the fifth.

At a hotel across the city from his last home he secured a room and went up to it immediately. Behind drawn blinds, masked keyhole, and closed transom, he took the money out again. He had intended finishing his counting—the flight across the city having rekindled his desire to know the extent of his wealth—but when he found that he had bunched it, had put already counted with uncounted, and thought of the immensity of the task, he gave it up. Counting was a "tough job," and the afternoon papers would tell him how much he had.

He wanted to look at the money, to feast his eyes upon it, to caress his fingers with it, but its abundance made him uneasy, frightened him even, notwithstanding that it was safe here from prying eyes. There was too much of it. It unnerved him. A thousand dollars, or perhaps even ten thousand, would have filled him with wild joy, but this bale. Furtively, he put it back in the valise.

For the first time now he thought of it not as money,—a thing in itself—but as money—potential women, cards, liquor, idleness, everything! It took his breath for the instant—the thought of the things the world held for him now! And he realized that he was wasting time, that these things were abroad, beckoning, while he stood in his room dreaming of them. He opened the valise and took out a double handful of the bills, cramming them into his pockets.

On the steps descending from the office to the street he halt-ed abruptly. A hotel of this sort—or any other—was certainly no place to leave a hundred and fifty thousand dollars unguarded. A fine chump he would be to leave it behind and have it stolen!

He hurried back to his room and, scarcely pausing to renew his former precautions, sprang to the valise. The money was still there. Then he sat down and tried to think of some way by which the money could be protected during his absence. He was hun-gry—he had not eaten since morning—but he could not leave the money. He found a piece of heavy paper, wrapped the money in it and lashed it securely, making a large but inconspicuous bundle.

On the street newsboys were shouting extras. Joe bought a paper, folded it carefully so that its headlines were out of sight, and went to a restaurant on First Avenue. He sat at a table back in one corner, with his bundle on the floor and his feet on the bundle. Then with elaborate nonchalance he spread the paper before him and read of the daylight holdup in which $250,000 had been taken from an automobile belonging to the Fourth National Bank. $250,000! He grabbed the bundle from the floor, knocking his forehead noisily against the table in his haste, and put it in his lap. Then he red-dened with swift self-consciousness, paled apprehensively, and yawned exaggeratedly. After assuring himself that none of the other men in the restaurant had noted his peculiar behavior, he turned his attention to the newspaper again.

Five of the bandits had been caught in the very act, the paper said, and two of them were seriously wounded. The bandits, who, according to the paper, must have had information concerning the unusually large shipment from some friend on the inside, had bungled their approach, bringing their own automobile to rest too far from their victim's for the greatest efficiency. Nevertheless, the sixth bandit had made away with the money. As was to lie expected, the bandits denied that there was a sixth, but the disappearance of the money testified irrefragably, to his existence.

From the restaurant Joe went to a saloon on Howard Street,

bought two bottles of white liquor, and took them to his room. He had decided that he would have to remain indoors that night; he couldn't walk around with $250,000 under his arm. Suppose some flaw in the paper should suddenly succumb to the strain upon it? Or he should drop the bundle?

He fidgeted about the room for hours, pondering his problem with all the concentration of which his dull mind was capable. He opened one of the bottles that he had brought, but he set it aside untasted. He could not risk drinking until he had safeguarded the money. It was too great a responsibility to be mixed with alcohol. The temptations of women and cards and the rest did not bother him now; time enough for them when the money was safe. He couldn't leave the money in his room, and he couldn't carry it to any of the places he knew, or to any place at all, for that matter.

He slept little that night, and by morning had made no headway against his problem. He thought of banking the money, but dismissed the thought as absurd. He couldn't walk into a bank a day or so after a widely advertised robbery and open an account with a bale of currency. He even thought of finding some secluded spot where he could bury it; but that seemed still more ridiculous. A few shovels of dirt was not sufficient protection. He might buy or rent a house and conceal the money on his own premises; but there were fires to consider, and what might serve as a hiding place for a few hundred dollars wouldn't do for many thousands. He must have an absolutely safe plan, one that would be safe in every respect and would admit of no possible loophole through which the money could vanish. He knew half-a-dozen men who could have told him what to do; but which of them could he trust where $250,000 was concerned?

When he was giddy from too much smoking on an empty stomach, he packed his valise again and left the hotel. A day of uneasiness and restlessness, with the valise ever in his hand or under his foot, brought no counsel. The gray-green incubus that his battered bag housed benumbed him, handicapped by his never-agile imagination. His nerves began to send little fluttering messages—forerunners of panic—to his brain.

Leaving a restaurant that evening he encountered Doc Haire himself.

"Hello, Joe! Going away?"

Joe looked down at the valise in his hand. "Yes," he said.

That was it! Why hadn't he thought of it before! In another city, at some distance from the scene of the robbery, none of the restrictions that oppressed him in Spokane would be present. Seattle, Portland, San Francisco, Los Angeles, the East!

Although he had paid for a berth, Joe Shupe did not occupy it; but sat all night in a day coach. At the last moment he had realized that the ways of sleeping-cars were unknown to him—perhaps one was required to surrender one's hand baggage. Joe did not know, but he did know that the money in his valise was not going to leave his hands.

In Seattle he gained no more liberty than he had had in Spokane. He had purposed to open an account with each bank in the city, distributing his wealth widely in cautious amounts; and for two days he tried to carry out his plan. But his nervous legs simply would not carry him through the door of a bank. There was something too austere, too official, too all-knowing, about the very architecture of these financial institutions, and there was no telling what complications, what questioning, awaited a man inside.

A fear of being bereft of his wealth by more cunning thieves—and he admitted frankly now that there might be many such—began to obsess him, and kept him out of dance hall, poolroom, gambling-house, and saloon. From anyone who addressed even the most casual of sentences to him he fled headlong. On his first day in Seattle he bought a complete equipment of bright and gaudy clothes, but he wore them for only half an hour. He felt that they gave him an altogether too affluent appearance, and would certainly attract the attention of thieves in droves.

At night now he slept with the valise in bed beside him, one of his arms bent over it in a protecting embrace that was not unlike a bridegroom's, waking now and then with the fear that someone was tugging at it. And every night it was a different hotel. He changed his lodgings each day, afraid of the curiosity his habit of always carrying the valise might arouse if he stayed too long in any one hotel.

Such intelligence as he was ordinarily in possession of was by this time completely submerged beneath the panic in which he lived. He went aimlessly about the city, a shabby man with the look of a harried rabbit in his furtive eyes, destinationless, without purpose, filled with forebodings that were now powerless except to deepen the torpor in his head.

A senseless routine filled his days. At eight or eight-thirty in the morning he would leave the hotel where he had slept, eat his breakfast at a nearby lunchroom, and then walk—down Second to Yessler Way, to Fourth, to Pike—or perhaps as far as Stewart—to Second, to Yessler Way, to Fourth. Sometimes he would desert his beat to sit for an hour or more on one of the green iron benches around the totem in Pioneer Square, staring vacantly at the street, his valise either at his side or beneath his feet. Presently, goaded by an obscure disquietude, he would get up abruptly and go back to his promenade along Yessler Way to Fourth, to Pike, to Second, to Yessler Way, to—

His nights were more vivid; with darkness his brain shook off some of its numbness and became sensitive to pain. Lying in the dark, always in a strange room, he would be filled with wild fears whose anarchic chaos amounted to delirium. Only in his dreams did he see things clearly. His brief and widely spaced naps brought him distinct, sharply etched pictures in which invariably he was robbed of his money, usually to the accompaniment of physical violence in its most unlovely forms.

The end was inevitable. In a larger city Joe Shupe might have gone on until his mentality had wasted away entirely and he collapsed. But Seattle is not large enough to smother the identities of its inhabitants; strangers' faces become familiar. One becomes accustomed to meeting the man in the brown derby somewhere in the vicinity of the post office, and the red-haired girl with the grapes on her hat somewhere along Pine Street between noon and one o'clock: and looks for the slim youth with the remarkable mustache, expecting to pass him on the street at least twice during the course of the day. And so it was that two plain-clothes men came to recognize Joe Shupe and his battered valise and his air of dazed fear.

They didn't take him very seriously at first, until, quite by accident, they grew aware of his custom of changing his address each night. Then one day, when they had nothing special on hand and when the memory of reprimands they had received from their superiors for not frequently enough "showing results" was fresh, they met Joe on the street. For two hours they shadowed him—up Fourth to Pike, to Second, to Yessler Way. On the third round trip, confusion and chagrin sent the officers to accost Joe.

"I ain't done nothing!" Joe told them, hugging the valise to his body with both arms. "You leave me be!"

One of the officers said something that Joe did not understand—he was beyond comprehending anything by now—but tears came from his red-rimmed eyes and ran down the hollows of his cheeks.

"You leave me be!" he repeated.

Then, still clasping the valise to his bosom, he turned and ran down the street. The officers easily overtook him.

Joe Shupe's story of how he had come into possession of the stolen quarter-million was received by everyone—police, press, and public—with a great deal of merriment. But, now that the responsibility for the money's safety rested with the Seattle police, he slept soundly that night, as well as those that followed; and when he appeared in the courtroom in Spokane two weeks later, to plead futilely that he was not one of the men who had held up the Fourth National Bank's automobile, he was his normal self again, both physically and mentally.

THE BLACK HAT THAT WASN'T THERE

"NOW LISTEN, Mr. Zumwalt, you're holding out on me; and it won't do! If I'm going to work on this case, I've got to have the whole story."

He looked thoughtfully at me for a moment through screwed-up blue eyes. Then he got up and went to the door of the outer office, opening it. Past him I could see the bookkeeper and the stenographer sitting at their desks. Zumwalt closed the door and returned to his desk, leaning across it to speak in a husky undertone.

"You are right, I suppose. But what I am going to tell you must be held in the strictest confidence."

I nodded, and he went on:

"About two months ago one of our clients, Stanley Gorham, turned $100,000 worth of bonds over to us. He had to go to the Orient on business, and he had an idea that the bonds might go over par during his absence; so he left them with us to be sold if they did. Yesterday I had occasion to go to the safe-deposit box where the bonds had been put—in the Golden Gate Trust Company's vault—and they were gone!'"

"Anybody except you and your partner have access to the box?"
"No."

"When did you see the bonds last?'"
"They were in the box the Saturday before Dan left. And one

of the men on duty in the vault told me that Dan was there the following Monday."

"All right! Now let me see if I've got it all straight. Your partner, Daniel Rathbone, was supposed to leave for New York on the twenty-seventh of last month, Monday, to meet an R. W. DePuy. But Rathbone came into the office that day with his baggage, and said that important personal affairs made it necessary for him to postpone his departure, that he had to be in San Francisco the following morning. But he didn't tell you what that personal business was.

"You and he had some words over the delay, as you thought it important that he keep the New York engagement on time. You weren't on the best of terms, having quarreled a couple of days before over a shady deal Rathbone had put over. And so you—"

"Don't misunderstand me," Zumwalt interrupted. "Dan had done nothing dishonest. It was simply that he had engineered several transactions that—well, I thought he had sacrificed ethics to profits."

"I see. Anyhow, starting with your argument over his not leaving for New York that day, you and he wound up by dragging in all your other differences, and practically decided to dissolve partnership as soon as it could be done. The argument was concluded in your house out on Fourteenth Avenue; and, as it was rather late by then and he had checked out of his hotel before he had changed his mind about going to New York, he stayed there with you that night."

"That's right," Zumwalt explained. "I have been living at a hotel since Mrs. Zumwalt has been away, but Dan and I went out to the house because it gave us the utmost privacy for our talk; and when we finished it was so late that we remained there."

"Then the next morning you and Rathbone came down to the office and—"

"No," he corrected me. "That is, we didn't come down here together. I came here while Dan went to transact whatever it was that had held him in town. He came into the office a little after noon, and said he was going East on the evening train. He sent Quimby, the bookkeeper, down to get his reservations and to check his baggage, which he had left in the office here overnight. Then Dan and I went to lunch together, came back to the office for a few minutes—he had some mail to sign—and then he left."

"I see. After that, you didn't hear from or of him until about ten days later, when DePuy wired to find out why Rathbone hadn't been to see him?"

"That's right. As soon as I got DePuy's wire, I sent one to Dan's brother in Chicago, thinking perhaps Dan had stopped over with him: but Tom wired back that he hadn't seen his brother. Since then I've had two more wires from DePuy. I was sore with Dan for keeping DePuy waiting, but still I didn't worry too much.

"Dan isn't a very reliable person, and if he suddenly took a notion to stop off somewhere between here and New York for a few days, he'd do it. But yesterday, when I found that the bonds were gone from the safe-deposit box and learned that Dan had been to the box the day before he left, I decided that I'd have to do something. But I don't want the police brought into it if it can be avoided.

"I feel sure that if I can find Dan and talk to him, we can straighten the mess out somehow without scandal. We had our differences, but I like him too well, for all his occasional wildness, to want to see him in jail. So I want him found with as much speed and as little noise as possible."

"Has he got a car?"

"Not now. He had one but he sold it five or six months ago."

"Where'd he bank? I mean his personal account?"

"At the Golden Gate Trust Company."

"Got any photos of him?"

"Yes."

He brought out two from a desk drawer—one full-face, and the other a three-quarter view. They showed a man in the middle of his life, with shrewd eyes set close together in a hatchet face, under dark, thin hair. But the face was rather pleasant for all its craftiness.

"How about his relatives, friends, and so on—particularly his feminine friends?"

"His only relative is the brother in Chicago. As to his friends: he probably has as many as any man in San Francisco.

"Recently he has been on very good terms with a Mrs. Earnshaw, the wife of a real-estate agent. She lives on Pacific Street, I think. I don't know just how intimate they were, but he used to call her up on the phone frequently, and she called him here nearly every day. Then there is a girl named Eva Duthie, a cabaret entertainer, who lives in the 1100 block of Bush Street."

"Have you looked through his stuff here?"

"Yes, but perhaps you'd like to look for yourself."

He led me into Rathbone's private office: a small box of a room, just large enough for a desk, a filing cabinet, and two chairs, with doors leading into the corridor, the outer office, and Zumwalt's.

"While I'm looking around you might get me a list of the serial numbers of the missing bonds," I said. "They probably won't help us right away, but we can get the Treasury Department to let us know when the coupons come in, and from where."

I didn't expect to find anything in Rathbone's office, and I didn't.

Before I left, I questioned the stenographer and the bookkeeper. They already knew that Rathbone was missing, but they didn't know that the bonds were gone too.

The girl—Mildred Narbett was her name—said that Rathbone had dictated a couple of letters to her on the twenty-eighth—the day he left for New York—both of which had to do with the partners' business; and told her to send Quimby to check his baggage and make his reservations. When she returned from lunch she had typed the two letters and taken them in for him to sign, catching him just as he was about to leave.

John Quimby, the bookkeeper, described the baggage he had checked: two large pigskin bags and a cordovan Gladstone bag. Having a bookkeeper's mind, he had remembered the number of the berth he had secured for Rathbone on the evening train—

lower 4, car 8. Quimby had returned with the checks and tickets while the partners were out at luncheon, and had put them on Rathbone's desk.

At Rathbone's hotel I was told that he had left on the morning of the twenty-seventh, giving up his room, but leaving his two trunks there, as he intended living there after his return from New York, in three or four weeks. The hotel people could tell me little worth listening to, except that he had left in a taxicab.

At the taxi stand outside I found the driver who had carried Rathbone.

"Rathbone? Sure, I know him!" he told me around a limp cigarette. "Yeah, I guess it was about that date that I took him down to the Golden Gate Trust Company. He had a coupla big yellow bags and a little brown one. He busted into the bank, carrying the little one, and right out again, looking like somebody had kicked him on his corns. Had me take him to the Phelps Building"—the offices of Rathbone & Zumwalt were in that building—"and didn't give me a jit over my fare!"

At the Golden Gate Trust Company I had to plead and talk a lot, but they finally gave me what I wanted—Rathbone had drawn out his account, a little less than $5,000, on the twenty-fifth of the month, the Saturday before he left town.

From the trust company I went down to the Ferry Building baggage-rooms and cigared myself into a look at the records for the twenty-eighth. Only one lot of three bags had been checked to New York that day.

I telegraphed the numbers and Rathbone's description to the Agency's New York office, instructing them to find the bags and, through them, find him.

Up in the Pullman Company's offices I was told that car "8" was a through car, and that they could let me know within a couple of hours whether Rathbone had occupied his berth all the way to New York.

On my way up to the 1100 block of Bush Street I left one of

Rathbone's photographs with a photographer, with a rush order for a dozen copies.

I found Eva Duthie's apartment after about five minutes of searching vestibule directories, and got her out of bed. She was an undersized blonde girl of somewhere between nineteen and twenty-nine, depending upon whether you judged by her eyes or by the rest of her face.

"I haven't seen or heard from Mr. Rathbone for nearly a month," she said. "I called him up at his hotel the other night—had a party I wanted to ring him in on—but they told me that he was out of town."

Then, in answer to another question:

"Yes, we were pretty good friends, but not especially thick. You know what I mean: we had a lot of fun together but neither of us meant anything to the other outside of that."

Mrs. Earnshaw wasn't so frank. But she had a husband, and that makes a difference. She was a tall, slender woman, as dark as a gypsy, with a nervous trick of chewing her lower lip.

We sat in a stiffly furnished room and she stalled me for about fifteen minutes, until I came out flat-footed with her.

"It's like this, Mrs. Earnshaw," I told her. "Mr. Rathbone has disappeared, and we are going to find him. You're not helping me and you're not helping yourself. I came here to get what you know about him.

"I could have gone around asking a lot of questions among your friends; and if you don't tell me what I want to know, that's what I'll have to do. And, while I'll be as careful as possible, still there's bound to be some curiosity aroused, some wild guesses, and some talk. I'm giving you a chance to avoid all that. It's up to you."

"You are assuming," she said coldly, "that I have something to hide."

"I'm not assuming anything. I'm hunting for information about Daniel Rathbone."

She bit her lip on that for a while, and then the story came out bit by bit, with a lot in it that wasn't any too true, but straight enough in the long run. Stripped of the stuff that wouldn't hold water, it went like this:

She and Rathbone had planned to run away together. She had left San Francisco on the twenty-sixth, going directly to New Orleans. He was to leave the next day, apparently for New York, but he was to change trains somewhere in the Middle West and meet her in New Orleans. From there they were to go by boat to Central America.

She pretended ignorance of his designs upon the bonds. Maybe she hadn't known. Anyhow, she had carried out her part of the plan, but Rathbone had failed to show up in New Orleans. She hadn't shown much care in covering her trail, and private detectives employed by her husband had soon found her. Her husband had arrived in New Orleans and had persuaded her to return home.

She wasn't a woman to take kindly to the jilting Rathbone had handed her, so she hadn't tried to get in touch with him.

Her story rang true enough, but just to play safe, I put out a few feelers in the neighborhood, and what I learned seemed to verify what she had told me. I gathered that few of the neighbors had made guesses that weren't a million miles away from the facts.

I got the Pullman Company on the telephone and was told that lower 4, car 8, leaving for New York on the twenty-eighth, hadn't been occupied at all.

Zumwalt was dressing for dinner when I went up to his room at the hotel where he was staying.

I told him all that I had learned that day, and what I thought.

"Everything makes sense up until Rathbone left the Golden Gate Trust Company vault on the twenty-seventh, and after that nothing does! He had planned to grab the bonds and elope with this Mrs. Earnshaw, and he had already drawn out of the bank all his own money. That's all orderly. But why should he have gone back to the office? Why should he have stayed in town that night? What was the important business that held him? Why should he have ditched Mrs. Earnshaw? Why didn't he use his reservations at least part of the way across the country, as he had planned? False trail, maybe, but a rotten one! There's nothing to do, Mr. Zumwalt, but to call in the police and the newspapers, and see what publicity and a nation-wide search will do for us."

"But that means jail for Dan!" he protested.

"It does, but it can't be helped. And remember, you've got to protect yourself. You're his partner, and while not criminally responsible, you are financially responsible for his actions. You've got to put yourself in the clear."

He nodded reluctant agreement and I grabbed the telephone.

For two hours I was busy giving all the dope we had to the police, and as much as we wanted published to the newspapers.

I sent off three telegrams. One to New York, asking that Rathbone's baggage be opened as soon as the necessary authority could be secured. (If he hadn't gone to New York the baggage should be waiting at the station.) One to Chicago, asking that Rathbone's brother be interviewed and then shadowed for a few days. And one to New Orleans, to have the city searched for him. Then I headed for home and bed.

News was scarce, and the papers the next day had Rathbone spread out all over the front pages, with photographs and descriptions and wild guesses and wilder clues that had materialized somehow within the short space between the time the newspapers got the story and the time they went to press.

I spent the morning preparing circulars and plans for having the country covered, and arranging to have steamship records searched.

Just before noon a telegram came from New York, itemizing the things found in Rathbone's baggage. The contents of the two large bags didn't mean anything. They might have been packed for use or for a stall. But the things in the Gladstone bag, which had been found unlocked, were puzzling.

Here's the list:

> Two suits silk pajamas, 4 silk shirts, 8 linen collars, 4 suits underwear, 6 neckties, 6 pairs sox, 18 handkerchiefs, 1 pair military brushes, 1 comb, 1 safety razor, 1 tube shaving cream, 1 shaving brush, 1 toothbrush, 1 tube tooth paste, 1 can talcum powder, 1 bottle hair tonic, 1 cigar case holding 12 cigars, 1 .32 Colt's revolver, 1 map of Honduras, 1 Spanish-English dictionary, 2 books postage stamps, 1 pint Scotch whiskey, and 1 manicure set.

Zumwalt, his bookkeeper, and his stenographer were watching two men from headquarters search Rathbone's office when I arrived there. After I showed them the telegram the detectives went back to their examination.

"What's the significance of that list?" Zumwalt asked.

"It shows that there's no sense to this thing the way it now stands," I said. "That Gladstone bag was packed to be carried. Checking it was all wrong—it wasn't even locked. And nobody ever checks Gladstone bags filled with toilet articles—so checking it for a stall would have been the bunk! Maybe he checked it as an afterthought—to get rid of it when he found he wasn't going to need it. But what could have made it unnecessary to him? Don't forget that it's apparently the same bag that he carried into the Golden Gate Trust Company vault when he went for the bonds. Blast it if I can dope it out!"

"Here's something else for you to dope out," one of the city detectives said, getting up from his examination of the desk and holding out a sheet of paper. "I found it behind one of the drawers, where it had slipped down."

It was a letter, written with blue ink in a firm, angular, and unmistakably feminine hand on heavy white notepaper.

Dear Dannyboy:

If it isn't too late, I've changed my mind about going. If you can wait another day, until Tuesday, I'll go. Call me up as soon as you get this, and if you still want me I'll pick you up in the roadster at the Shattuck Avenue Station on Tuesday afternoon.

More than ever yours,

"Boots"

It was dated the twenty-sixth—the Sunday before Rathbone had disappeared.

"That's the thing that made him lay over another day, and made him change his plans," one of the police detectives said. "I guess we better run over to Berkeley and see what we can find at the Shattuck Avenue Station."

"Mr. Zumwalt," I said, when he and I were alone in his office, "how about this stenog of yours?"

He bounced up from his chair and his face turned red.

"What about her?"

"Is she—How friendly was she with Rathbone?"

"Miss Narbett," he said heavily, deliberately, as if to be sure that I caught every syllable, "is to be married to me as soon as my wife gets her divorce. That is why I canceled the order to sell my house. Now, would you mind telling me just why you asked ?"

"Just a random guess!" I lied, trying to soothe him. "I don't want to overlook any bets. But now that's out of the way."

"It is," he was still talking deliberately, "and it seems to me that most of your guesses have been random ones. If you will have your office send me a bill for your services to date, I think I can dispense with your help."

"Just as you say. But you'll have to pay for a full day today; so, if you don't mind, I'll keep on working at it until night."

"Very well! But I am busy, and you needn't bother about coming in with any reports."

"All right," I said, and bowed myself out of the office.

That letter from "Boots" had *not* been in the desk when I searched it. I had taken every drawer out and even tilted the desk to look under it. The letter was a plant!

Suppose (I thought, walking up Market Street, bumping shoulders and stepping on people's feet) the two partners were in this thing together. One of them would have to be the goat, and that part had fallen to Rathbone. Zumwalt's manner and actions since his partner's disappearance fit that theory. Employing a private detective before calling in the police was a good play. In the first place, it gave him the appearance of innocence. Then the private dick would tell him everything he learned, every step he took, giving Zumwalt an opportunity to correct any mistakes or oversights in the partners' plans before the police came into it; and if the private detective got on dangerous ground he could be called off.

And suppose Rathbone was found in some city where he was unknown—and that would be where he'd go. Zumwalt would volunteer to go forward to identify him. He would look at him and say, "No, that's not him." Rathbone would be turned loose, and that would be the end of that trail.

This theory left the sudden change in Rathbone's plans unaccounted for; but it made his return to the office on the afternoon of the twenty-seventh more plausible. He had come back to confer with his partner over that unknown necessity for the change, and they had decided to leave Mrs. Earnshaw out of it. Then they had gone out to Zumwalt's house. For what? And why had Zumwalt decided not to sell the house? And why had he taken the trouble to give me an explanation? Could they have cached the bonds there?

A look at the house wouldn't be a bad idea.

I telephoned Bennett, at the Oakland Police Department.

"Do me a favor, Frank? Call Zumwalt on the phone. Tell him you've picked up a man who answers Rathbone's description to a T; and ask him to come over and take a look at him. When he gets there, stall him as long as you can—pretending that the man is being fingerprinted and measured, or something like that—and then tell him that you've found that the man isn't Rathbone, and that you are sorry to have brought him over there, and so on. If you only hold him for half or three-quarters of an hour it'll be enough—it'll take him more than half an hour traveling each way. . . . Thanks!"

I stopped in at the office, stuck a flashlight in my pocket, and headed for Fourteenth Avenue.

Zumwalt's house was a two-story, semi-detached one; and the lock on the front door held me up about four minutes. A burglar would have gone through it without checking his stride. This breaking into the house wasn't exactly according to the rules, but on the other hand, I was legally Zumwalt's agent until I discontinued work that night—so this crashing-in couldn't be considered illegal.

I started at the top floor and worked down. Bureaus, dressers, tables, desks, chairs, walls, woodwork, pictures, carpets, plumbing—I looked at everything that was thick enough to hold paper. I didn't take things apart, but it's surprising how speedily you can go through a house when you're in training.

I found nothing in the house itself, so I went down into the cellar.

It was a large cellar and divided in two. The front part was paved with cement, and held a full coal-bin, some furniture, some canned goods, and a lot of odds and ends of housekeeping accessories. The rear division, behind a plaster partition where the steps ran down from the kitchen, was without windows, and illuminated only by one swinging electric light, which I turned on.

A pile of lumber filled half the space; on the other side barrels and boxes were piled up to the ceiling; two sacks of cement lay beside them, and in another corner was a tangle of broken furniture. The floor was of hard dirt.

I turned to the lumber pile first. I wasn't in love with the job ahead of me—moving the pile away and then back again. But I needn't have worried

A board rattled behind me, and I wheeled to see Zumwalt rising from behind a barrel and scowling at me over a black automatic pistol.

"Put your hands up," he said.

I put them up. I didn't have a pistol with me, not being in the habit of carrying one except when I thought I was going to need it; but it would have been all the same if I had a pocket full of them. I don't mind taking chances, but there's no chance when you're looking into the muzzle of a gun that a determined man is holding on you.

So I put my hands up. And one of them brushed against the swinging light globe. I drove my knuckles into it. As the cellar went black, I threw myself backward and to one side. Zumwalt's gun streaked fire.

Nothing happened for a while. I found that I had fallen across the doorway that gave to the stairs and the front cellar. I figured that I couldn't move without making a noise that would draw lead; so I lay still.

Then began a game that made up in tenseness what it lacked in action.

The part of the cellar where we were was about twenty by twenty feet, and blacker than a new shoe. There were two doors. One, on the opposite side, opened into the yard and was, I supposed, locked. I was lying on my back across the other, waiting for a pair of legs to grab. Zumwalt, with a gun out of which only one bullet had been spent, was somewhere in the blackness, and aware, from his silence, that I was still alive.

I figured I had the edge on him. I was closest to the only practicable exit; he didn't know that I was unarmed; he didn't know whether I had help close by or not. Time was valuable to him, but not necessarily so to me. So I waited.

Time passed. How much I don't know. Maybe half an hour.

The floor was damp and hard and thoroughly uncomfortable. The electric light had cut my head when I broke it, and I couldn't determine how badly I was bleeding. I thought of Tad's "blind man in a dark room hunting for the black hat that wasn't there," and knew how he felt.

A box or barrel fell over with a crash—knocked over by Zumwalt, no doubt, moving out from his hiding-place.

Silence for a while. And then I could hear him moving cautiously off to one side.

Without warning two streaks from his pistol sent bullets into the partition somewhere above my feet.

Silence again, and I found that I was wet and dripping with perspiration. I could hear his breathing, but couldn't determine whether he was nearer or was breathing more heavily.

Then a soft, sliding, dragging across the dirt floor . . . I pictured him crawling awkwardly on his knees and one hand, the other hand holding the pistol out ahead of him—the pistol that would spit fire as soon as its muzzle touched something soft. And I became uneasily aware of my bulk. I am thick through the waist; and there in the dark it seemed to me that my paunch must extend almost to the ceiling—a target no bullet could miss.

I stretched my hands out toward him and held them there. If they touched him first I'd have a chance.

He was panting harshly now; and I was breathing through a mouth that was stretched as wide as it would go, so that there would be no rasping of the large quantities of air I was taking in and letting out.

Abruptly he came.

Hair brushed the fingers of my left hand. I closed them about it, pulling the head I couldn't see viciously toward me, driving my right fist beneath it. I put everything I had in that smack.

He wiggled, and I hit him again.

Then I was sitting astride him, my flashlight hunting for his pistol. I found it, and yanked him to his feet.

As soon as his head cleared I herded him into the front cellar and got a globe to replace the one I had smashed.

"Now dig it up," I ordered.

That was a safe way of putting it. I wasn't sure what I wanted or where it would be, except that his selecting this part of the cellar to wait for me in made it look as if this was the right place.

"You'll do your own digging!" he growled.

"Maybe,'" I said, "but I'm going to do it now, and I haven't time to tie you up. So if I've got to do the digging, I'm going to crown you first, so you'll sleep peacefully until it's all over."

All smeared with blood and dirt and sweat, I must have looked capable of anything, for when I took a step toward him and clenched my fist, he gave in.

From behind the lumber pile he brought a spade, moved some of the barrels to one side, and started turning up the dirt.

When a hand—a man's hand—dead-yellow where the damp dirt didn't stick to it—came into sight I stopped him.

I had found "it," and I had no stomach for looking at "it" after three weeks of lying in the wet ground....

In court, Lester Zumwalt's plea was that he had killed his partner in self-defense. Zumwalt testified that he had taken the Gorham bonds in a futile attempt to recover losses in the stock market; and that when Rathbone—who had intended taking them and going to Central America with Mrs. Earnshaw—had visited the safe-deposit box and found them gone, he had returned to the office and charged Zumwalt with the theft.

At that time Zumwalt had not suspected his partner's own dishonest plans, and had promised to restore the bonds. They had gone to Zumwalt's house to discuss the matter; and Rathbone, dissatisfied with his partner's plan of restitution, had attacked Zumwalt, and had been killed in the ensuing struggle.

Then Zumwalt had told Mildred Narbett, his stenographer, the whole story and had persuaded her to help him. Between them they had made it appear that Rathbone had been in the office for a while the next day—the twenty-eighth—and had left for New York.

However, the jury seemed to think that Zumwalt had lured his partner out to the Fourteenth Avenue house for the purpose of killing him; so Zumwalt was found guilty of murder in the first degree.

The first jury before which Mildred Narbett was tried disagreed. The second jury acquitted her, holding that there was nothing to show that she had taken part in either the theft of the bonds or the murder, or that she had any knowledge of either crime until afterward; and that her later complicity was, in view of her love for Zumwalt, not altogether blameworthy.

THE SECOND-STORY ANGEL

CARTER BRIGHAM—Carter Webright Brigham in the tables of contents of various popular magazines—woke with a start, passing from unconsciousness into full awareness too suddenly to doubt that his sleep had been disturbed by something external.

The moon was not up and his apartment was on the opposite side of the building from the streetlights; the blackness about him was complete—he could not see so far as the foot of his bed.

Holding his breath, not moving after that first awakening start, he lay with straining eyes and ears. Almost at once a sound—perhaps a repetition of the one that had aroused him—came from the adjoining room: the furtive shuffling of feet across the wooden floor. A moment of silence, and a chair grated on the floor, as if dislodged by a careless shin. Then silence again, and a faint rustling as of a body scraping against the rough paper of the wall.

Now Carter Brigham was neither a hero nor a coward, and he was not armed. There was nothing in his rooms more deadly than a pair of candlesticks, and they—not despicable weapons in an emergency—were on the far side of the room from which the sounds came.

If he had been awakened to hear very faint and not often repeated noises in the other room—such rustlings as even the most adept burglar might not avoid—the probabilities are that Carter would have been content to remain in his bed and try to frighten the burglar away by yelling at him. He would not have disregarded the fact that in an encounter at close quarters under these conditions every advantage would lie on the side of the prowler.

But this particular prowler had made quite a lot of noise, had even stumbled against a chair, had shown himself a poor hand at stealthiness. That an inexpert burglar might easily be as dangerous as an adept did not occur to the man in the bed.

Perhaps it was that in the many crook stories he had written, deadliness had always been wedded to skill and the bunglers had always been comparatively harmless and easily overcome, and that he had come to accept this theory as a truth. After all, if a man says a thing often enough, he is very likely to acquire some sort of faith in it sooner or later.

Anyhow, Carter Brigham slid his not unmuscular body gently out from between the sheets and crept on silent bare feet toward the open doorway of the room from which the sounds had come. He passed from his bed to a position inside the next room, his back against the wall beside the door during an interlude of silence on the intruder's part.

The room in which Carter now stood was every bit as black as the one he had left; so he stood motionless, waiting for the prowler to betray his position.

His patience was not taxed. Very soon the burglar moved again, audibly; and then against the rectangle of a window—scarcely lighter than the rest of the room—Carter discerned a man-shaped shadow just a shade darker coming toward him. The shadow passed the window and was lost in the enveloping darkness.

Carter, his body tensed, did not move until he thought the burglar had had time to reach a spot where no furniture intervened. Then, with clutching hands thrown out on wide-spread arms, Carter hurled himself forward.

His shoulder struck the intruder and they both crashed to the floor. A forearm came up across Carter's throat, pressing into it.

He tore it away and felt a blow on his cheek. He wound one arm around the burglar's body, and with the other fist struck back. They rolled over and over across the floor until they were stopped by the legs of a massive table, the burglar uppermost.

With savage exultance in his own strength, which the struggle thus far had shown to be easily superior to the other's, Carter twisted his body, smashing his adversary into the heavy table. Then he drove a fist into the body he had just shaken off and scrambled to his knees, feeling for a grip on the burglar's throat. When he had secured it he found that the prowler was lying motionless, unresisting. Laughing triumphantly, Carter got to his feet and switched on the lights.

The girl on the floor did not move.

Half lying, half hunched against the table where he had hurled her, she was inanimate. A still, twisted figure in an austerely tailored black suit—one sleeve of which had been torn from the shoulder—with an unended confusion of short chestnut hair above a face that was linen-white except where blows had reddened it. Her eyes were closed. One arm was outflung across the floor, the other lay limply at her side; one silken leg was extended, the other folded under her.

Into a corner of the room her hat, a small black toque, had rolled; not far from the hat lay a very small pinch-bar, the jimmy with which she had forced an entrance.

The window over the fire escape—always locked at night—was wide-open. Its catch hung crookedly.

Mechanically, methodically—because he had been until recently a reporter on a morning paper, and the lessons of years are not unlearned in a few weeks—Carter's eyes picked up these details and communicated them to his brain while he strove to conquer his bewilderment.

After a while his wits resumed their functions and he went over to kneel beside the girl. Her pulse was regular, but she gave no other indications of life. He lifted her from the floor and carried her to the leather couch on the other side of the room. Then he brought cold water from the bathroom and brandy from the bookcase. Generous applications of the former to her temples and face and of the latter between her lips finally brought a tremor to her mouth and a quiver to her eyelids.

Presently she opened her eyes, looked confusedly around the room, and endeavored to sit up. He pressed her head gently down on the couch.

"Lie still a moment longer—until you feel all right."

She seemed to see him then for the first time, and to remember where she was. She shook her head clear of his restraining hand and sat up, swinging her feet down to the floor.

"So I lose again," she said, with an attempt at nonchalance that was only faintly tinged with bitterness, her eyes meeting his.

They were green eyes and very long, and they illuminated her face which, without their soft light, had seemed of too sullen a cast for beauty, despite the smooth regularity of the features.

Carter's glance dropped to her discolored cheek, where his knuckles had left livid marks.

"I'm sorry I struck you," he apologized. "In the dark I naturally thought you were a man. I wouldn't have—"

"Forget it," she commanded coolly. "It's all in the game."

"But I—"

"Aw, stop it!" Impatiently. "It doesn't amount to anything. I'm all right."

"I'm glad of that."

His bare toes came into the range of his vision, and he went into his bedroom for slippers and a robe. The girl watched him silently when he returned to her, her face calmly defiant.

"Now," he suggested, drawing up a chair, "suppose you tell me all about it."

She laughed briefly. "It's a long story, and the bulls ought to be here any minute now. There wouldn't be time to tell it."

"The police?"

"Uh-huh."

"But I didn't send for them! Why should I?"

"God knows!" She looked around the room and then abruptly straight into his eyes. "If you think I'm going to buy my liberty, brother"—her voice was icy insolent—"you're way off!"

He denied the thought. Then: "Suppose you tell me about it."

"All primed to listen to a sob story?" she mocked. "Well, here goes: I got some bad breaks on the last couple of jobs I pulled and had to lay low—so low that I didn't even get anything to eat for a day or two. I figured I'd have to pull another job for getaway money—so I could blow town for a while. And this was it! I was sort of giddy from not eating and I made too much noise; but even at that"—with a scornful laugh—"you'd never have nailed me if I'd had a gun on me!"

Carter was on his feet.

"There's food of some sort in the icebox. We'll eat before we do any more talking."

A grunt came from the open window by which the girl had entered. Both of them wheeled toward it. Framed in it was a burly, red-faced man who wore a shiny blue serge suit and a black derby hat. He threw one thick leg over the sill and came into the room with heavy, bearlike agility.

"Well, well"—the words came complacently from his thick-lipped mouth, under a close-clipped gray mustache—"if it ain't my old friend Angel Grace!"

"Cassidy!" the girl exclaimed weakly, and then relapsed into sullen stoicism.

Carter took a step forward.

"What—"

"'S all right!" the newcomer assured him, displaying a bright badge. "Detective-Sergeant Cassidy. I was passin' and sported somebody makin' your fire escape. Decided to wait until they left and nab 'em with the goods. Got tired of waitin' and came up for a look-see."

He turned jovially to the girl.

"And here it turns out to be the Angel herself! Come on, kid, let's take a ride."

Carter put out a detaining hand as she started submissively toward the detective.

"Wait a minute! Can't we fix this thing up? I don't want to prosecute the lady."

Cassidy leered from the girl to Carter and back, and then shook his head.

"Can't be done! The Angel is wanted for half a dozen jobs. Don't make no difference whether you make charges against her or not—she'll go over for plenty anyways."

The girl nodded concurrence.

"Thanks, old dear," she told Carter, with an only partially successful attempt at nonchalance, "but they want me pretty bad."

But Carter would not submit without a struggle. The gods do not send a real flesh-and-blood feminine crook into a writer's rooms every evening in the week. The retention of such a gift was worth contending for. The girl must have within her, he thought, material for thousands, tens of thousands, of words of fiction. Was that a boon to be lightly surrendered? And then her attractiveness was in itself something; and a still more potent claim on his assistance—though not perhaps so clearly explainable—was the mottled area his fists had left on the smooth flesh of her cheek.

"Can't we arrange it somehow?" he asked. "Couldn't we fix it so that the charges might be—er—unofficially disregarded for the present?"

Cassidy's heavy brows came down and the red of his face darkened.

"Are you tryin' to—"

He stopped, and his small blue eyes narrowed almost to the point of vanishing completely.

"Go ahead! You're doin' the talkin'."

Bribery, Carter knew, was a serious matter, and especially so when directed toward an officer of the law. The law is not to be lightly set aside, perverted, by an individual. To fling to this gigantic utensil a few bits of green-engraved paper, expecting thus to turn it from its course, was, to say the least, a foolhardy proceeding.

Yet the law as represented by this fat Cassidy in baggy, not too immaculate garments, while indubitably the very same law, seemed certainly less awe-inspiring, less unapproachable. Almost it took on a human aspect—the aspect of a man who was not entirely without his faults. The law just now, in fact, looked out through little blue eyes that were manifestly greedy, for all their setting in a poker face.

Carter hesitated, trying to find the words in which his offer would be most attractively dressed; but the detective relieved him of the necessity of broaching the subject.

"Listen, mister," he said candidly. "I get you all right! But on the level, I don't think it'd be worth what it'd cost you."

"What would it cost?"

"Well, there's four hundred in rewards offered for her that I know of—maybe more."

Four hundred dollars! That was considerably more than Carter had expected to pay. Still, he could get several times four hundred dollars' worth of material from her.

"Done!" he said. "Four hundred it is!"

"Woah!" Cassidy rumbled. "That don't get me nothin'! What kind of chump do you think I am? If I turn her in I get that much, besides credits for promotion. Then what the hell's the sense of me turnin' her loose for that same figure and runnin' the risk of bein' sent over myself if it leaks out?" Carter recognized the justice of the detective's stand.

"Five hundred," he bid.

Cassidy shook his head emphatically.

"On the level, I wouldn't touch it for less'n a thousan'—and you'd be a sucker to pay that much! She's a keen kid all right, but the world's full of just as keen ones that'll come a lot cheaper."

"I can't pay a thousand," Carter said slowly; he had only a few dollars more than that in his bank.

His common sense warned him not to impoverish himself for the girl's sake, warned him that the payment of even five hundred dollars for her liberty would be a step beyond the limits of rational conduct. He raised his head to acknowledge his defeat, and to tell Cassidy that he might take the girl away; then his eyes focused on the girl. Though she still struggled to maintain her attitude of ironic indifference to her fate, and did attain a reckless smile, her chin quivered and her shoulders were no longer jauntily squared.

The dictates of reason went for nothing in the face of these signs of distress.

Without conscious volition, Carter found himself saying, "The best I can do is seven hundred and fifty."

Cassidy shook his head briskly, but he caught one corner of his lower lip between his teeth, robbing the rejecting gesture of its finality.

The girl, stirred into action by the detective-sergeant's indecision, put an impulsive hand on his arm and added the weight of her personality to the temptation of the money.

"Come on, Cassidy," she pleaded. "Be a good guy—give me a break! Take the seven fifty! You got rep enough without turning me in!"

Cassidy turned abruptly to Carter. "I'm makin' a sap o' myself, but give me the dough!"

At the sight of the check book that Carter took from a desk drawer, Cassidy balked again, demanding cash. Finally they persuaded him to accept a check made payable to "Cash."

At the door he turned and wagged a fat finger at Carter.

"Now remember," he threatened, "if you try any funny business on this check I'm going to nail you if I have to frame you to do it!"

"There'll be no funny business," Carter assured him.

There was no doubt of the girl's hunger; she ate ravenously of the cold beef, salad, rolls, pastry, and coffee that Carter put before her. Neither of them talked much while she ate. The food held her undivided attention, while Carter's mind was busy planning how his opportunity might be utilized to the utmost.

Over their cigarettes the girl mellowed somewhat, and he persuaded her to talk of herself. But clearly she had not accepted him without many reservations, and she made no pretence of lowering her guard.

She told him her story briefly, without going into any details.

"My old man was named John Cardigan, but he was a lot better known as 'Paper-Box John,' from his trick of carrying his tools around in an unsuspicious-looking shoebox. If I do say it myself, he was as slick a burglar as there was in the grift! I don't remember Ma very well. She died or left or something when I was a little kid and the old man didn't like to talk about her.

"But I had as good a bringing up, criminally speaking, as you ever heard of. There was the old man, a wizard in his line; and my older brother Frank—he's doing a one-to-fourteen-year stretch in Deer Lodge now—who wasn't a dub by any means with a can opener—safe-ripping, you know. Between them and the mobs they ran with, I got a pretty good education along certain lines.

"Everything went along fine, with me keeping house for the old man and Frank, and them giving me everything I wanted, until the old man got wiped out by a night watchman in Philly one night. Then, a couple weeks later, Frank got picked up in some burg out in Montana—Great Falls. That put me up against it. We hadn't saved much money—easy come, easy go—and what we had I sent out to Frank's mouthpiece—a lawyer—to try to spring him. But it was no go—they had him cold, and they sent him over.

"After that I had to shift for myself. It was a case of either cashing in on what the old man and Frank had taught me or going on the streets. Of course, I wouldn't have had to go on the streets actually—there were plenty of guys who were willing to take me in—it's just that it's a rotten way of making a living. I don't want to be owned!

"Maybe you think I could have got a job somewhere in a store or factory or something. But in the first place, a girl with no experience has a hard time knocking down enough jack to live on; and then again, half the dicks in town know me as the old man's daughter, and they wouldn't keep it a secret if they found me working any place—they'd think I was getting a job lined up for some mob.

"So, after thinking it all over, I decided to try the old man's racket. It went easy from the first. I knew all the tricks and it wasn't hard to put them into practice. Being a girl helped, too. A couple times, when I was caught cold, people took my word for it that I had got into the wrong place by mistake.

"But being a girl had its drawbacks, too. As the only she-burglar in action, my work was sort of conspicuous, and it wasn't long before the bulls had a line on me. I was picked up a couple times, but I had a good lawyer, and they couldn't make anything stick, so they turned me loose; but they didn't forget me.

"Then I got some bad breaks, and pulled some jobs that they knew they could tie on me; and they started looking for me proper. To make things worse, I had hurt the feelings of quite a few guys who had tried to get mushy with me at one time or another, and they had been knocking me—saying I was up-stage and so on— to everybody, and that hadn't helped me any with the people who might have helped me when I was up against it.

"So besides hiding from the dicks I had to dodge half the guns in the burg for fear they'd put the finger on me—turn me up to the bulls. This honor among thieves stuff doesn't go very big in New York!

"Finally it got so bad that I couldn't even get to my room, where my clothes and what money I had were. I was cooped up in a hangout I had across town, peeping out at dicks who were watching the joint, and knowing that if I showed myself I was a goner.

"I couldn't keep that up, especially as I had no food there and couldn't get hold of anybody I could trust; so I took a chance tonight and went over the roof, intending to knock over the first likely-looking dump I came to for the price of some food and a ducat out of town.

"And this was the place I picked, and that brings my tale up to date."

They were silent for a moment, she watching Carter out of the corners of her eyes, as if trying to read what was going on in his mind, and he turning her story around in his head, admiring its literary potentialities.

She was speaking again, and now her voice held the slightly metallic quality that it had before she had forgotten some of her wariness in her preoccupation with her story.

"Now, old top, I don't know what your game is; but I warned you right off the reel that I wasn't buying anything."

Carter laughed. "Angel Grace, your name suits you—heaven must have sent you here," he said, and then added, a little self-consciously, "My name is Brigham—Carter Webright Brigham."

He paused, half expectantly, and not in vain.

"Not the writer?"

Her instantaneous recognition caused him to beam on her—he had not reached the stage of success when he might expect everyone to be familiar with his name.

"You've read some of my stuff?" he asked.

"Oh, yes! 'Poison for One' and 'The Settlement' in Warner's Magazine, 'Nemesis, Incorporated' in the National, and all your stories in Cody's!"

Her voice, even without the added testimony of the admiration that had replaced the calculation in her eyes, left no doubt in his mind that she had indeed liked his stories.

"Well, that's the answer," he told her. "That money I gave Cassidy was an investment in a gold mine. The things you can tell me will fairly write themselves and the magazines will eat 'em up!"

Oddly enough, the information that his interest had been purely professional did not seem to bring her pleasure; on the contrary, little shadows appeared in the clear green field of her eyes.

Seeing them, Carter, out of some intuitive apprehension, hastened to add: "But I suppose I'd have done the same even if you hadn't promised stories—I couldn't very well let him carry you off to jail."

She gave him a sceptical smile at that, but her eyes cleared.

"That's all very fine," she observed, "as far as it goes. But you mustn't forget that Cassidy isn't the only sleuth in the city that's hunting for me. And don't forget that you're likely to get yourself in a fine hole by helping me."

Carter came back to earth.

"That's right! We'll have to figure out what is the best thing to do."

Then the girl spoke: "It's a cinch I'll have to get out of town! Too many of them are looking for me, and I'm too well-known. Another thing: you can trust Cassidy as long as he hasn't spent that money, but that won't be long. Most likely he's letting it go over a card table right now. As soon as he's flat he'll be back to see you again. You'll be safe enough so far as he's concerned—he can't prove anything on you without giving himself away—but if I'm where he can find me he'll pinch me unless you put up more coin; and he'll try to find me through you. There's nothing to it but for me to blow town."

"That's just what we'll do," Carter cried. "We'll pick out some safe place not far away, where you can go today. Then I'll meet you there tomorrow and we can make some permanent arrangements."

It was late in the morning before their plans were completed.

Carter went to his bank as soon as it was open and withdrew all but sufficient money to cover the checks he had out, including the one he had given the detective-sergeant. The girl would need money for food and fare, and even clothing, for her room, she was confident, was still watched by the police.

She left Carter's apartment in a taxicab, and was to buy clothes of a different color and style from those she was wearing and whose description the police had. Then she was to dismiss the taxicab and engage another to drive her to a railroad station some distance from the city—they were afraid that the detectives on duty at the railroad stations in the city, and at the ferries, would recognize her in spite of the new clothes. At the distant station she would board a train for the upstate town they had selected for their rendezvous.

Carter was to join her there the following day.

He did not go down to the street door with her when she left, but said goodbye in his rooms. At the leave-taking she shed her coating of worldly Cynicism and tried to express her gratitude.

But he cut her short with an embarrassed mockery of her own earlier admonition: "Aw, stop it!"

Carter Brigham did not work that day. The story on which he had been engaged now seemed stiff and lifeless and altogether without relation to actuality. The day and the night dragged along, but no matter how slowly, they did pass in the end, and he was stepping down from a dirty local train in the town where she was to wait for him.

Registering at the hotel they had selected, he scanned the page of the book given over to the previous day's business. "Mrs. H. H. Moore," the name she was to have used, did not appear thereon. Discreet inquiries revealed that she had not arrived.

Sending his baggage up to his room, Carter went out and called at the two other hotels in the town. She was at neither. At a newsstand he bought an armful of New York papers. Nothing about her arrest was in them. She had not been picked up before leaving the city, or the newspapers would have made much news of her.

For three days he clung obstinately to the belief that she had not run away from him. He spent the three days in his New York rooms, his ears alert for the ringing of the telephone bell, examining his mail frantically, constantly expecting the messenger, who didn't come. Occasionally he sent telegrams to the hotel in the upstate town—futile telegrams.

Then he accepted the inescapable truth: she had decided—perhaps had so intended all along—not to run the risk incidental to a meeting with him, but had picked out a hiding place of her own; she did not mean to fulfil her obligations to him, but had taken his assistance and gone.

Another day passed in idleness while he accustomed himself to the bitterness of this knowledge. Then he set to work to salvage what he could. Fortunately, it seemed to be much. The bare story that the girl had told him over the remains of her meal could with little effort be woven into a novelette that should be easily marketed. Crook stories were always in demand, especially one with an authentic girl-burglar drawn from life.

As he bent over his typewriter, concentrating on his craft, his disappointment began to fade. The girl was gone. She had treated him shabbily, but perhaps it was better that way. The money she had cost him would come back with interest from the sale of the serial rights of this story. As for the personal equation: she had been beautiful, fascinating enough—and friendly—but still she *was* a crook. . . .

For days he hardly left his desk except to eat and sleep, neither of which did he do excessively.

Finally the manuscript was completed and sent out in the mail. For the next two days he rested as fully as he had toiled, lying abed to all hours, idling through his waking hours, replacing the nervous energy his work always cost him.

On the third day a note came from the editor of the magazine to which he had sent the story, asking if it would be convenient for him to call at two-thirty the next afternoon.

Four men were with the editor when Carter was ushered into his office. Two of them he knew: Gerald Gulton and Harry Mack, writers like himself. He was introduced to the others: John Deitch and Walton Dohlman. He was familiar with their work, though he had not met them before; they contributed to some of the same magazines that bought his stories.

When the group had been comfortably seated and cigars and cigarettes were burning, the editor smiled into the frankly curious faces turned toward him.

"Now we'll get down to business," he said. "You'll think it a queer business at first, but I'll try to mystify you no longer than necessary."

He turned to Carter. "You wouldn't mind telling us, Mr. Brigham, just how you got hold of the idea for your story *The Second-Story Angel,* would you?"

"Of course not," Carter said. "It was rather peculiar. I was roused one night by the sound of a burglar in my rooms and got up to investigate. I tackled him and we fought in the dark for a while. Then I turned on the lights and—"

"And it was a woman—a girl!" Gerald Fulton prompted hoarsely.

Carter jumped.

"How did you know?" he demanded.

Then he saw that Fulton, Mack, Deitch, and Dohlman were all sitting stiffly in their chairs and that their dissimilar faces held for the time identical expressions of bewilderment.

"And after a while a detective came in?"

It was Mack's voice, but husky and muffled.

"His name was Cassidy!"

"And for a price things could be fixed," Deitch took up the thread.

After that there was a long silence, while the editor pretended to be intrigued by the contours of a hemispherical glass paperweight on his desk, and the four professional writers, their faces beet-red and sheepish, all stared intently at nothing.

The editor opened a drawer and took out a stack of manuscripts.

"Here they are," he said. "I knew there was something wrong when within ten days I got five stories that were, in spite of the differences in treatment, unmistakably all about the same girl!"

"Chuck mine in the wastebasket," Mack instructed softly, and the others nodded their endorsement of that disposition. All but Dohlman, who seemed to be struggling with an idea. Finally he addressed the editor.

"It's a pretty good story, at that, isn't it, all five versions?"

The editor nodded.

"Yes, I'd have bought one, but five—"

"Why not buy one? We'll match coins—"

"Sure, that's fair enough," said the editor.

It was done. Mack won.

Gerald Fulton's round blue eyes were wider than ever with a look of astonishment. At last he found words.

"My God! I wonder how many other men are writing that same story right now!"

But in Carter's mind an entirely different problem was buzzing around.

Lord! I wonder if she kissed this whole bunch, too!

WHEN LUCK'S RUNNING GOOD

A SHRIEK, unmistakenly feminine, and throbbing with terror, pierced the fog. Phil Truax, hurrying up Washington Street, halted in the middle of a stride and became as motionless as the stone apartment buildings that flanked the street.

The shriek swelled, with something violinlike in it, and ended with a rising inflection. Half a block away the headlights of two automobiles, stationary and oddly huddled together, glowed in the mist. Silence, a guttural grunt, and the shriek again . . . but now it held more anger than fear, and broke off suddenly.

Phil remained motionless. Whatever was happening ahead was none of his business, and he was a meddler in other people's affairs only when assured of profit therefrom. And, too, he was not armed. Then he thought of the $400 in his pocket: his winnings in the poker game he had just left. He had been lucky thus far tonight: mightn't his luck carry him a little further if he gave it the opportunity? He pulled his hat down firmly on his head and ran towards the lights.

The fog aided the headlights in concealing from him whatever was happening in the machines as he approached them, but he noticed that the engine of at least one was running. Then he skirted one of them, a roadster, checking his momentum by catching hold of a mudguard. For a fraction of a second he hung there, while dark eyes burned into his from a white face half hidden under a brawny hand.

Phil hurled himself on the back of the man to whom the hand belonged; his fingers closed around a sinewy throat. A white flame seared his eyeballs; the ground went soft and billowy under his feet, as if it were part of the fog. Everything—the burning eyes, the brawny hand, the curtains of the automobile—rushed toward him . . .

Phil sat up on the wet paving and felt his head. His fingers found a sore, swelling area running from above the left ear nearly to the crown. Both automobiles were gone. No pedestrians were in sight. Lights were shining through a few windows; forms were at many windows; and curious voices were calling questions into the fog.

Mastering his nausea, he got unsteadily to his feet, though his desire was to lie down again on the cool, damp street. Hunting for his hat, he found a small handbag and thrust it into his pocket. He recovered his hat from the gutter, tilted it to spare the bruise, and set out for home, ignoring the queries of the pajamaed spectators.

Dressed for bed, and satisfied that the injury to his head was superficial, Phil turned his attention to the souvenir of his adventure. It was a small bag of black silk, trimmed with silver beads, and still damp from its contact with the street.

He dumped the contents on the bed, and a bundle of paper money caught his eye. He counted the bills and found they totaled $355. Pushing the bills into the pocket of his bathrobe, he grinned. "Four hundred I win and three hundred and fifty I get for a tap on the head—a pretty good night!"

He picked up the other articles, looked at them, and returned them to the bag. A gold pencil, a gold ring with an opal set in it, a woman's handkerchief with a gray border and an unrecognizable design in one corner, a powder-box, a small mirror, a lipstick, some hairpins, and a rumpled sheet of note-paper covered with strange, exotic characters.

He smoothed out the paper and examined it closely, but could make nothing out of it. Some Asiatic language, perhaps. He took the ring from the bag again and tried to estimate its value. His knowledge of gems was small, but he decided that the ring could not be worth much—not more than $50 at the most. Still, $50 is $50. He put the ring with the money, lit a cigarette, and went to bed.

Phil awoke at noon. His head was still tender to the touch, but the swelling had gone. He walked downtown, bought early editions of the afternoon papers, and read them while he ate breakfast. He found no mention of the struggle on Washington Street, and the "Lost and Found" columns held nothing pertaining to the bag. That night he played poker until daylight and won $240. In an all-night lunchroom he read the morning papers. Still nothing of the struggle, but in the classified section of the *Chronicle:*

LOST—Early Tuesday morning, Lady's black silk bag trimmed with silver, containing money, ring, gold pencil, letter, etc. Finder may keep money if other articles are returned to CHRONICLE OFFICE.

He grinned, then frowned, and stared speculatively at the advertisement. The ring couldn't be worth three hundred dollars. He took it from his pocket, shielding it with a hand from the chance look of anyone in the lunchroom. No—$50 would be a big price. The pencil, powder-box, and lipstick case were of gold; but $150, say, would more than replace everything in the bag. The undecipherable letter remained—that must be the important item! A struggle between a woman and some men at four in the morning, nothing about it in the newspapers, a lost bag containing a paper covered with foreign characters, and then this generous offer—it might mean almost anything!

Of course, the wisest plan would be either to disregard the advertisement and keep what he had found, or to accept this offer and send everything but the money to the *Chronicle.* Either way would be playing it safe; but when a man's luck is running good he should crowd it to the limit.

Times come, as every gambler knows, when a man gets into a

streak of luck, when everything he touches proves fruitful; and his play then is to push his luck to a fare-you-well—make a killing while the fickle goddess is smiling.

He thought of the men he had known who had paid for their timidity in the face of Chance's favor—men who had won dollars where they might have won thousands, men who were condemned to be pikers all their lives through lack of courage to force their luck when it ran strong, an inability to rise with their stars.

"And my luck's running good," he whispered to the ring in his hand. "A thousand smackers in two days, after the long dry spell I've been through."

He returned the ring to his pocket and reviewed the chain of incidents leading up to the advertisement. Two facts that had lurked in his subconsciousness came out to face him: the shrieking voice had been musical even in its terror, and the eyes that had burned into his had been very beautiful.

He made up his mind as he finished his coffee.

"I'll sit in this racket, whatever it is, for a little while, anyway; and see what I can get myself."

At ten o'clock that morning Phil telephoned the office of the *Chronicle*, told the girl to whom he talked that he had found the bag but would return it to no one but its owner, and went back to bed.

At two o'clock he got up and dressed. He returned the ring to the bag, with everything except the money, and went into the kitchen to prepare breakfast. He usually went out for his meals, but today he wanted to be sure that he would not miss whoever might telephone or call. He had scarcely finished his meal when the doorbell rang.

"Mr. Traux?"

Phil nodded and invited the caller in. The man who entered the flat was about forty years old, nearly as tall as Phil, and perhaps twenty-five pounds heavier. He was fastidiously groomed in clothes of a European cut, and a walking-stick was crooked over one arm.

He accepted a chair with a polite smile, and said, "I shall take but a moment of your time. It is about the bag that I have come. The newspaper informed me you had found it."

He betrayed his foreignness more by the precision of his enunciation than by any accent.

"It is your bag?" Phil asked with just a hint of a chuckle.

The caller's red lips parted, baring twin rows of even white teeth.

"It is my niece's, but I can describe it. A black silk bag of about this size"—indicating with his small, shapely hands—"trimmed with silver, and holding between three and four hundred dollars, a gold pencil, a ring—an opal ring—a letter written in Russian, and the powder and rouge accessories that one would expect to find in a young woman's bag. Perhaps a handkerchief with her initial in Russian on it. That is the one you found?"

'It might be, Mr.—?

"Pardon me, sir!" The visitor extended a card. "Kapaloff, Boris Kapaloff."

Phil took the card and pretended to scrutinize it while he marshalled his thoughts. He was far from certain that he cared to force himself into this man's affairs. The man's whole appearance—the broad forehead slanting down from the roots of the crisp black hair to bulge a little just above the brows; the narrow, widely spaced eyes of cold hazel; the aquiline nose with a pronounced flare to the nostrils; the firm, too-red lips; the hard line of chin and jaw—evidenced a nature both able and willing to hold its own in any field.

And while Phil considered himself second to no man in guile, he knew that his intrigues had heretofore been confined to the world of tinhorn gamblers, ward-heelers, and such small fry. Small schooling for a game with this man whose voice, appearance, and poise proclaimed a denizen of a greater, more subtle world. Of course, if some decided advantage could be gained at the very outset . . .

"Where was the bag lost?" Phil asked.

The Russian's poise remained undisturbed.

'That would be most difficult to say," he replied in his cultured, musical voice. "My niece had been to a dance, and she carried several friends to their homes before returning to hers. The bag may have dropped from the car anywhere along the way."

A temptation to speak of the struggle on Washington Street came to Phil but he put it aside. Kapaloff might have been present that morning but it was obvious that he did not recognize Phil. The bag could have been found by someone who passed the spot later.

Phil decided to leave Kapaloff in doubt on that point for as long as possible, and he was further urged to postpone the clash that might ensue by a faint fear of coming to a showdown with this suave Russian. Nothing would be lost by waiting . . .

Kapaloff allowed a gentle impatience to tinge his manner. "Now about the bag?"

"The three hundred and fifty-five dollars is reward?" Phil asked. Kapaloff sighed ruefully.

"I am sorry to say it is. Ridiculous, of course, but perhaps you know something of young women. My niece was very fond of the opal ring—a trinket, worth but little. Yet no sooner did she discover her loss than she telephoned the newspaper office and offered the money as reward. Ridiculous! A hundred dollars would be an exaggerated value to place upon everything in the bag. But having made the offer, we shall have to abide by it."

Phil nodded. Kapaloff was lying—no doubt of that—but he wasn't the sort that one baldly denounces. Phil fidgeted and found himself avoiding his visitor's eyes. Then a wave of self-disgust flooded him. "Here I am," he thought, "letting this guy bluff me in my own flat, just because he has a classy front."

He looked into Kapaloff's hazel eyes and asked with perfect casualness, keeping every sign of what was going on in his brain out of his poker-player's face: "And how did the scrap in the automobile come out? I didn't see the end of it."

"I am so glad you said that!" Kapaloff cried, his face alight with joyous relief. "So very glad! Now I can offer my apologies for my childish attempts at deception. You see, I wasn't sure that you had seen the unfortunate occurrence—you could have found the bag later—although I was told that someone had tried to interfere. You were not injured seriously?" His voice was weighted with solicitude.

None of the bewilderment, chagrin, recognition of defeat that raged in Phil's brain showed in his face. He tried to match the other's blandness. "Not at all. A slight headache next morning, a sore spot for a few hours—nothing to speak of."

"Splendid!" Kapaloff exclaimed. "Splendid! And I want to thank you for your attempt to assist my niece, even though I must assure you it was most fortunate you were unsuccessful. We certainly owe you an explanation—my niece and I—and if you will bear with me I shall try not to take up too much of your time with it. We are Russians—my niece and I—and when the Czar's government collapsed, our place in our native land was gone. Kapaloff was not our name then; but what is a title after the dynasty upon which it depends and the holdings accruing to it are gone? What we endured between the beginning of the revolution and our escape from Russia I pray may never come to another!"

A cloud touched his face with anguish, but he brushed it away with a gesture of one delicate hand.

"My niece saw her father and her fiancé struck down within ten minutes. For months after that the real world did not exist for her. She lived in a nightmare. We watched her night and day for fear that she would succeed in her constant efforts to destroy herself. Then, gradually, she came back to us. For six months she has been, we thought, well. The alienists assured us that she was permanently cured.

"And then, late Monday night, she found between the pages of an old book a photograph of Kondra—he was her betrothed—and the poor child's mind snapped again. She fled from the house, crying that she must go back to Petrograd, to Kondra. I was out, but my valet and my secretary followed her, caught her somewhere in the city, and returned with her. The roughness with which your gallantry was met—for that I must beg your forgiveness. Serge and Mikhail have not yet learned to temper their zeal. To them I am still 'His Excellency,' in whose service anything may be done."

Kapaloff stopped, as if waiting for Phil's comment, but Phil was silent. His brain was telling him, over and over, "This bird has got you licked! The generosity of the reward isn't accounted for by this tale, but it will be before he's through."

His genial eyes still on Phil's Kapaloff fulfilled the prophecy. "After my niece was safely home and I heard what had happened, I had the advertisement put in the paper. It seemed the most promising way of learning the extent of the injury of the man who had tried to aid my niece. If he were unhurt and had found the bag, he would turn it over to the *Chronicle*, and the three hundred and fifty dollars would be little enough reward for his trouble. On the other hand, if he was seriously injured he would use the advertisement to get in touch with me and I could take further steps to provide for him. If the bag were found by someone else I would remain in ignorance; but you will readily understand that I had no desire to have my niece's distressing plight paraded before the public in the newspapers."

He paused, waiting again for Phil to speak.

When the pause had become awkward Phil shifted in his chair and asked, "And your niece—how is she now?"

"Apparently well again. I called a physician as soon as she returned. She was given an opiate and awoke that afternoon as if nothing unusual had happened. It may be that she will never be troubled again."

Phil started to get up from his chair to get the bag. There seemed to be no tangible reason for doubting the Russian's story—except that he did not want to believe it. But was the story flawless?

He relaxed in the chair again. If the tale were true, would Kapaloff have dictated the advertisement so that the bag would be delivered to the *Chronicle*? Wouldn't he have wanted to interview the finder?

The Russian was waiting for Phil to speak, and Phil had nothing to say. He wanted time to think this affair over carefully, away from the glances of the hazel eyes that were lancet-keen for all their blandness.

"Mr. Kapaloff," he said hesitantly, "here is how all this stands with me: I saw the bag's owner and found it under—well—funny circumstances. Not," he interjected quickly, as Kapaloff's eyebrows rose, "that your explanation is hard to believe; but I want to be sure I'm doing the right thing. So I'll have to ask you either to let me deliver the bag to your niece, or to go to the police, tell our stories, and let them straighten it out."

Kapaloff appeared to turn the offers over in his mind. Then he objected: "Neither alternative is inviting. The first would subject my niece to an embarrassing interview, and so soon after her trouble. The second—you should appreciate my distaste for the publicity that would follow the police's entry into the affair."

"I'm sorry, but—" Phil began, but Kapaloff cut him short by rising to his feet, smiling genially, with outstretched hand.

"Not at all, Mr. Truax. You are a man of judgment. In your position I should probably act in like manner. Can you accompany me to call upon my niece now?"

Phil stood up and grasped the dainty hand extended to him, and though the Russian's grip was light enough Phil could feel the swell of powerful muscles under the soft skin.

"I'm sorry," Phil lied, "but I have an engagement within half an hour. Perhaps you and your niece will be in the neighborhood within a few days and will find it convenient to call for it?"

He did not intend dealing with this man on alien ground.

"That will do nicely. Shall we say at three tomorrow?"

Phil repeated, "At three tomorrow," and Kapaloff bowed himself out.

Alone, Phil sat down and tried to torture his brain into giving him the solution of this puzzle; but he made little headway. Except in two minor instances the Russian's story had been impregnable. And those two details—the fact that he did not want the police dragged into the affair, and the fact that he had worded the advertisement so as to retain his anonymity behind the screen of the newspaper—were not, on close examination, conclusive.

On the other hand, insanity was notorious as a mask for villainy. How many crimes had been committed by use of the pretext that the victim, or the witnesses, were insane!

Kapaloff's manner had been candid enough and his poise had survived every twist of the situation, but . . . It was upon this last that Phil hung his doubts. "If that bird had contradicted me just once I'd believe him, maybe; but he was too damned agreeable!"

Phil returned home early that night. The cards had failed to hold him, now that his mind was occupied with what threatened to be a larger, more intricate game. He puzzled over the letter in Russian, but its characters meant nothing to his eyes. He tried to think of someone who could translate it for him; but the only Russian he knew was not a man to be trusted under any circumstances. He tried to read a magazine, but soon gave it up and crawled into bed, to toss about, smoke numerous cigarettes, and finally drop off to sleep.

The least expert of burglars would have laughed at the difficulty and resultant noise with which the two men opened the door of Phil's flat; but not the most desperate of criminals would have found anything laughable in their obvious determination. They were bent upon getting into the flat, and the racket incidental to their bungling attacks on the lock disconcerted them not at all. It was quickly evident they would force an entrance even if it were necessary to batter the door down.

Finally the lock succumbed, but by that time Phil was flattened behind his bathroom door, with a pistol in his hand and a confident grin on his face. The crudeness of the work on the lock eliminated whatever doubts he had had of his ability to take care of himself.

The outer door swung open but no light came through. The hall light had been extinguished. The hinges creaked a little, but Phil, peering through the slit between the bathroom door and the jamb, could see nothing. A whisper and an answer told him that there were at least two burglars. However noisy the men had been with the door, they were silent enough now. A slight rustling and then silence.

Not knowing where the men were, Phil did not move. A faint click sounded in the bedroom, and a weak, brief reflection from a flashlight showed an empty passageway.

Phil moved soundlessly toward the bedroom. As he reached the door the flashlight went on again and stayed on, its beam fixed on the empty bed. Phil snapped on the lights.

The two men standing beside the bed, one on either side, wheeled in unison and took a step forward, to halt before the menace of the weapon in Phil's hand. The men were very similar in appearance: the same bullet heads, the same green eyes under tangled brows, the same sullen mouths and high, broad cheekbones. But the one who held a blackjack in a still uplifted hand was heavier and broader than the other, and the bridge of his nose was dented by a dark scar that ran from cheek to cheek, just under his eyes.

For perhaps two seconds the men stood still. Then the larger man shrugged his enormous shoulders and grunted a syllable to his companion. The momentary confusion left their faces, to be replaced by looks of resolve as they advanced toward Phil.

His brain was racing. Kapaloff's "secretary and valet," of course; and as their indifference to the noises they had made at the door testified to their determination to do what they had come to do at any cost, so now did their indifference to the pistol in Phil's hand. Close to him as they were, he could hardly expect to drop both of them; but even if he did—the whole story would be bound to come out in the police investigation that must follow, and his chance of getting greater profit out of the affair would be blasted.

As the two men, working together like twin parts of a machine, contracted their muscles to spring, Phil hit on the way out. He leaped backward through the bedroom door, whirled, and jumped into the hall, shouting, "Help! Police!"

There was a snarling at the door, a scuffling, and the noise of two men running through the dark hall toward the front door. The laughter that welled up in Phil's throat silenced his shouts; he fired his pistol into the floor and returned to his bedroom.

He laid a chair gently on its side and swept some books and papers from the table to the floor. Then he turned with a wide-eyed semblance of excitement to welcome the callers in various degrees of negligé who came in answer to his bellowing. After a while a policeman came and Phil told his story.

"A noise woke me up and I saw a man in the room. I grabbed my gun and yelled at him, but I forgot to take the safety catch off the gun." With sham sheepishness: "I guess I was kind of scared. He ran out in the hall with me after him. I remembered the safety, then, and took a shot at him, but it was too dark to see whether I hit him. I looked through my stuff and don't think he got anything, so I guess no harm's done."

After the last question had been answered and the last caller had gone, Phil bolted the door and shook hands with himself. "Well, that fixes Mr. Kapaloff's story. And you've got him faded, my boy, so don't let me catch you letting him run a bluff on you again."

At five minutes past three on Thursday afternoon the Kapaloffs arrived. Romaine Kapaloff acknowledged her uncle's introduction in easy and faultless English, and thanked Phil warmly for his efforts in her behalf Tuesday morning.

Phil found himself holding her hand and straining his self-possession to the utmost to keep from gaping and stammering. The girl—she couldn't have been more than nineteen—was looking up through brown eyes that glowed now with Phil's gray ones and asking: "And you really weren't hurt?"

To Phil she seemed the loveliest creature he had ever seen. His attempts at extortion seemed mean and sordid. Because he was bitterly ashamed of his attempt to wring profits from her uncle, and was badly rattled, he answered almost gruffly; and in his effort to keep the chaos within him from his face he made a mask of stupidity.

"Not at all. Really! It was nothing."

Kapaloff stood watching them with the smile of one who sees his difficulties dissipated. Finally their hands fell apart and they sought chairs. There was an awkward pause. Phil knew that though they sat there until nightfall he could not bring up the question of the girl's sanity, demand the corroboration of her uncle's story, which was the excuse for the meeting.

Kapaloff said nothing, sat smiling benignly on girl and boy. The girl glanced at her uncle, as if expecting him to open the conversation, but when he ignored her silent appeal she turned impulsively to Phil, putting out her hand.

"Uncle Boris told you about my—about the trouble?"

Phil nodded, started to reach for the extended hand, thought better of it, and twined his fingers together between his knees.

"Then you know how fortunate it was that your gallantry wasn't successful. I can't understand why you didn't laugh at Uncle Boris' story—it must have sounded fantastic to you. But—Oh, it is horrible! I can never trust myself again, no matter what the doctors say!"

Phil found that he was holding her hand, after all. He looked at Kapaloff, who was smiling sympathetically. Phil and the girl stood up, and for an instant her eyes held a baffling undertone of pleading. Then it was gone, and she was turning to her uncle.

Phil had but one idea in his mind now: to hand over the bag, get rid of these people, and be alone with his shame and disgust. He moved toward the door.

"I'll get the bag," he said in a tired, weak voice.

A silver purse that dangled from the girl's wrist clattered to the floor. As Phil turned his head at the sound, Kapaloff bent to pick up the purse, and Romaine Kapaloff's eyes met Phil's. For an infinitesimal part of a second her eyes burned into his as they had Tuesday morning, and stark terror wiped out the smooth young beauty of her face.

Then her uncle was holding out the purse, her face was composed again, and Phil was walking toward his bedroom door with the blood pounding in his temples. He sat on the top of his trunk, gnawed at a thumbnail, and thought desperately. Then he took the bag from the trunk and thrust it under his coat and returned to his guests.

"It is gone."

Kapaloff's urbanity seemed about to desert him. His face darkened and he took a swift step forward. Then he was master of himself again, and was asking pleasantly, "Are you positive?"

"You may look if you like."

Phil went to the telephone and a few seconds later was talking to the desk sergeant at the precinct station.

"A burglar got in here last night. One of your men was in afterward, and I told him I hadn't missed anything. Now I find that a lady's handbag is gone . . . All right."

He turned from the telephone to the Kapaloffs.

"I woke up some time this morning and found two burglars in the room. They escaped, and I thought everything was safe. I forgot about the bag, and didn't look to see if it was still here. I'm sorry."

Neither of the Kapaloff's gave any indication of previous knowledge of the burglary. Boris Kapaloff said evenly, "Very unfortunate, but the bag and its contents were not so valuable that we should worry unduly over the loss."

"I am going to the police station this afternoon to give a description of the bag. Shall I tell them that it is your property and have them turn it over to you?"

"If you will be so kind. Our address is Lajolla Avenue, Burlingame."

Conversation lagged. Several times Kapaloff seemed about to speak, but each time he restrained himself. The girl's eyes, when Phil met them, held a question which he made no attempts to answer.

The Kapaloffs departed. Phil shook hands with both of them, answering the girl's unspoken question with a quick pressure.

When they were gone, he withdrew the bag, counted $355 from

the bills in his pocket, and put the money in the bag. Then he drew a deep breath. That was the end of three years of searching for an "easy living."

Since his discharge from the army he had been drifting, finding himself at odds with the world, gambling, doing chores for political clubs—never doing anything very vicious, perhaps, but steadily becoming more and more enmeshed in the underworld. As he looked back now, with the memory of his shame and self-disgust of a few minutes ago still fresh, he thought that he would not feel quite so worthless if there had been some outstanding crime in his past, instead of a legion of petty deeds.

Well, that was all past! After this tangle came to an end he would get a job and go back to the ways he had known before the war interrupted his aspirations.

He wrapped the bag in heavy paper, tied it, and sealed it securely. Then he took it downtown and turned it over to the friendly proprietor of a poolroom to be put in the safe.

For two days Phil kept to his rooms—days in which he sprang to the telephone at the first tingling of the bell. He tried to reach Romaine Kapaloff by telephone, got her house, and was told by a harsh voice in broken English that she was not at home. Three times he tried it, but the results were always the same. Then he tried to talk to her uncle, and got the same answer.

On the second night he slept hardly at all. He would doze and then spring into wakefulness, imagining that the bell had sounded, race to the telephone, to be asked, "What number are you calling?"

Then he decided to wait no longer. When a man's luck is running good he should force the issue—not wait in idleness until his fortunes turn . . .

In Burlingame, Phil easily found the Kapaloffs' house. At the first garage where he inquired, the name was unknown, but they knew where "the Russians" lived. Even in the dark he had no difficulty in recognizing the house from the garageman's description.

He drove past it, left his borrowed car in the darkest shadow he could find, and turned afoot. The building loomed immense in the night, a great gray structure set in a park, ringed by a tall iron fence overgrown with hedging. The nearest house was at least half a mile away.

No light came from the house, and Phil found the front gate locked. He crossed the road and squatted under a tree some two hundred feet away. His plan involved nothing further than waiting in the vicinity until he saw Romaine, found some means of communicating with her, or found an avenue through which his luck could carry him toward a solution of whatever mystery existed in the house across the road.

The chances were that Romaine was a prisoner; otherwise she would have got word to him before this. His watch registered 10:15.

He waited.

When his watch said 1:30 his youth and his faith in his luck overcame his patience. A man might as well be home in bed as sitting out here waiting for something to turn up. When a man's luck is running good . . .

He skirted the hedge-grown fence until he found a tree with a branch that grew over the barrier. He climbed the tree, crawled out on the overhanging limb, swung for a minute, and dropped.

He landed on hands and knees in soft, moist loam. Carefully he moved forward, keeping a cluster of bushes between himself and the house. When he reached the bushes he halted. Nothing that might serve to conceal him was between the bushes and the building, and he was afraid to trust himself out in the pale starlight

Again he waited.

Three-quarters of an hour passed, and then he heard the sound of metal scraping against wood. He could see nothing. The sound came again and he identified it: someone was opening a shutter, cautiously, stopping at each sound the bolt made.

A babel of dogs' voices broke out at the rear of the house, and around the corner swept a pack of great hounds, to throw themselves frenziedly against one of the lower windows.

Phil heard the shutter slam sharply. In the wake of the dogs a man stumbled. The shutter opened again and Kapaloff leaned out to speak to the man in the yard. Above the men's words Phil heard Romaine Kapaloff's voice, raised in anger. In the rectangle of light shining from the window six wolfhounds were twisting and leaping—not the sedate, finely bred borozois of my lady's promenade, but great, shaggy wolfkillers of the steppes, over half a man's height from ground to shoulder, and more than a hundred pounds each of fighting machinery.

Phil held his breath, shrunk behind his screen, and prayed that what he had heard somewhere of those wolf-hounds hunting by sight and not by scent be true, that his presence escape their noses.

Kapaloff withdrew his head and closed the shutter. The man in the yard shouted at the dogs. They followed him to the rear of the house. A door closed, shutting off the dogs' voices. Phil was damp with perspiration, but he knew now that the dogs were kept indoors.

From an upper story came a muffled scream and the sound of something falling against a shutter. Then silence. The sound had come from the front of the house, Phil decided—the corner room on the third floor, at a guess.

For a moment Phil was tempted to leave the place and enlist the services of the police; but he was not used to allying himself with the police—on the few occasions when he had had dealings with the law he had found it on the other side. Then, too, would not the glib Kapaloff have the advantage of his aristocratic manner, his standing as a property holder, and his seemingly secure position in the world?

Against all this Phil would have only his bare word and a vague story, backed by three years of living without what the police call "visible means of support." He could imagine what the outcome would be. He would have to play this out alone.

He left the protecting bush and crept to the front of the house. Around the corner he paused to scan the building. So far as he could determine in the dark every window was fitted with a shutter. He was afraid to try the shutters on the first floor; but it was unlikely that one of them would have been left unbolted.

The upper windows held out the best promise of an entrance. He crept up on the porch, removed his shoes, and stuck them in his hip pockets. Mounting the porch rail, he encircled a pillar with arms and legs and pulled himself up until his fingers caught the edge of the porch roof. Silently he drew himself up and lay face down on the shingles. No sound came from house or grounds. On hands and knees he went to each of the four windows and tried the shutters. All were securely fastened.

He sat up and studied the third-story windows. The window on the extreme left should open into the room from which the last noises had come—Romaine Kapaloff's room, if his reasoning was correct. A rainspout ran up the corner of the house, within arm's length of the window. If the spout would support him, he could reach the window and risk a signal to the girl. He crawled over and inspected the spout, testing it with his hands. It shook a bit but he decided to risk it.

He found a niche for the stockinged toes of one foot, drew himself up, reached for a higher hold on the spout with his hands, and felt for a support for the other foot. There was a tearing noise, a rattle of tin, and Phil thumped to the roof of the porch with a length of pipe in his hands.

He rolled over, let go the spout, and caught at the roof in time to keep from going over the edge. The released piece of tin hit the roof with a clang and rolled over the edge to clatter madly on the paved walk.

The night was suddenly filled with the snarling of hounds. The pack careened around the corner, flung themselves against the porch, tore up and down the yard—lithe, evil shapes in the starlight, with flashing, dripping jaws. Peeping over the edge of the roof, Phil saw a man following the dogs, and a gleam of metal in the man's hands.

A sound came from behind Phil. A second-story shutter was

being opened. He wormed his way to it and lay on his back under it, close to the wall. The shutter swung open and a man leaned out—the man with the scarred face.

Phil lay motionless, not breathing, his body tense, a forefinger tight around the trigger of his pistol, the pistol's muzzle not six inches from the body slanting over him.

The man called a question to the one in the yard. The front door opened and Kapaloff's easy voice sounded. The man at the window and the one in the yard called to Kapaloff in Russian; he answered.

Then the man at the window withdrew, his footsteps receded, and a door closed within the room. The window remained open. Phil was over the sill in an instant, and in the dark room. As his feet touched the floor he sensed something amiss, heard a grunt, and lunged blindly forward. The room filled with dancing lights, and there was a roaring in his ears . . .

Phil awoke with his nostrils stinging from ammonia administered by the man with the scarred face. Phil tried to push the bottle away, but his hands were lashed. His feet, too, were tied.

He looked around, turning his head from side to side. He was lying on a bed in a luxuriously furnished chamber, fully clothed except for coat and shoes.

Kapaloff stood across the room, looking on with a smile of mild mockery. On one side of the bed stood the man with the scar; on the opposite side, the other man who had entered Phil's flat. At a word from Kapaloff this man assisted Phil to a sitting position.

Phil's head ached cruelly; but taking his cue from Kapaloff, he tried to keep his face composed, as if he found nothing disconcerting in his position. Kapaloff came over to the bed and asked solicitously, "You are not seriously injured this time either, I trust?"

"I don't think so. But if these hired men of yours keep it up they'll wear my head away."

Kapaloff exhibited his teeth in an affable smile. "You are the fortunate possessor of a tough head. But I hope it will not prove as little amenable to persuasion as it has been to force."

Phil said nothing. Every iota of his will was needed to keep his face calm. The pain in his head was unbearable. Kapaloff went on talking, his voice a mixture of friendliness and banter.

"Your tenacity in clinging to the bag would, under other circumstances, be admirable; but really it must be terminated. I must insist that you tell me where it is."

"Suppose my head stays tough on the inside, too?" Phil suggested.

"That would be most unfortunate. But you are going to be reasonable, aren't you? When you stumbled into this affair you saw, or suspected, much that did not appear on the surface—being an extremely perspicacious young man—and thought you could unearth whatever was hidden and exact a little—well, not blackmail, perhaps, though a crude intellect might call it that. Now you must see that I have the advantage; and assuredly you are enough the sportsman to acknowledge defeat, and make what terms you can."

"And what are the terms?"

"Turn the bag over to me and sign a few papers."

"Papers for what?"

"Oh, the papers are unimportant, merely a precaution. You will not know what they contain exactly—just a few statements, supposedly made by you: confessions to certain crimes, perhaps—to insure me that you will not trouble the police afterward. I am frank. I do not know where you have put the bag. After you so obligingly entered the window that Mikhail left open for you, Mikhail and Serge visited your rooms again. They found nothing. So I offer terms. The bag, your signature, and you receive five hundred dollars, exclusive of the money that was in the bag."

"Suppose I don't like the terms?"

"That would be most unfortunate," Kapaloff protested. "Serge"—motioning toward the man who had helped Phil sit up—"is remarkably adept with a heated knife; and remembering the ludicrous manner in which you put him and Mikhail to rout, I fancy he would relish having you as a subject for his playfulness."

Phil turned his head and pretended to look at Serge, but he scarcely saw the man. He was trying to convince himself that this threat was a bluff, that Kapaloff would not dare resort to torture; but his success was slight. If his ability to read men was of any value at all then this Russian was one who would stop at nothing to attain his ends.

Phil decided he would not submit to any excruciating pain to save the bag. In the first place, he did not know how valuable the paper might be; secondly, he seemed to be the girl's only ally, and he flattered himself that he was more valuable an aid than a letter could be. However, he would fight to the last inch—bluff until the final moment.

"I can't make terms until I talk with your niece."

Kapaloff expostulated gently but firmly. "That is not possible. I am sorry, but you must understand that my position is very delicate, and I cannot permit it to become more complicated."

"No talk, no terms," Phil said flatly.

Kapaloff let his distress furrow his brow. "Think it over. You must know that I shall not be pleased by the necessity of making you suffer. In fact"—with a whimsical smile—"Serge will be the only participant who will enjoy it."

"Bring on the knife," Phil said coolly. "No talk, no terms."

Kapaloff nodded to Serge, who left the room.

"There is no hurry—a few minutes' delay doesn't matter," Kapaloff urged. "Consider your position. Think! Under Serge's skilled hands you will tell—do not doubt it—but then you lose the extra five hundred dollars, besides causing me no little anguish—to say nothing of your own plight."

Phil's smile matched Kapaloff's for affability. "It would be just wasting time. If I can't see Miss Kapaloff, I'll stand put."

Serge returned with an alcohol lamp and a small poniard. He set the lamp on the table, lit it, and held the blade in the flame.

Phil watched the preparations with a face that was tranquil. He noticed, suddenly, that the hand holding the poniard trembled, and, raising his eyes, he saw tiny globules of moisture glistening on Serge's forehead. His face was haggard, with white lines around the mouth.

Mikhail put Phil down on the bed again, gripping his ankles firmly. Phil said nothing. He was beginning to enjoy himself— knowing that he could stop the whole thing with a word. Serge's knees were trembling noticeably now; and Mikhail's fingers around Phil's ankles jerked and were moist with perspiration.

Phil grinned and spoke banteringly to Kapaloff. "You should rehearse these men of yours. I bet their torturing is no better than their burglary."

Kapaloff chuckled good-naturedly. "But you must consider that a bungling torturer may obtain effects that are beyond a skilled one."

Then Serge came to the bed, the poniard glowing in his shaking hand.

Phil spoke casually, "If you don't mind, I'd like to sit up and watch this."

"Certainly!" Kapaloff himself assisted him to a sitting position. "Is there anything else I can do to make it more bearable?"

"Thanks, no. I can manage nicely now."

Serge was extending the heated dagger toward the soles of Phil's feet, from which Mikhail had removed the stockings. The blade was wavering in the man's nervous hands; his eyes were bulging, and his face was wet with perspiration. Mikliail's fingers were pressing into Phil's ankles, grinding the flesh painfully; both of Kapaloff's assistants were breathing hoarsely.

Phil forced himself to disregard the pain of Mikhail's grip, and smiled derisively. The point of the poniard was within an inch of his feet. Then Serge let it fall to the floor, and shrank back from the bed. Kapaloff spoke to him. Slowly Serge stooped for the poniard, and went to the lamp to reheat it, his body quivering as with ague.

He came to the bed again, his teeth clenched behind taut, bloodless lips. He bent over the bed, and Phil felt the heat of the approaching blade. Lazily he glanced at Kapaloff, carrying his acting to its pinnacle just before surrendering.

Then, with a choking cry, Serge flung the poniard from him and dropped on his knees before Kapaloff, pleading pitifully. Kapaloff answered with exaggerated gentleness, as one would speak to an infant. Serge got to his feet slowly, and backed away, his head hanging. One of Kapaloff's hands came out of his pocket, holding a pistol. The pistol spat flame. Serge caught both hands to his body, and crumpled to the floor.

Kapaloff walked unhurriedly to where the man had fallen, put the toe of one trim shoe under Serge's shoulder, and turned him over on his back. Then, the pistol hanging loosely at his side, he sent four bullets into Serge's face, wiping out the features in a red smear.

Kapaloff turned and looked, with eyes that held nothing but polite expectation, at Mikhail. Mikhail had released Phil's ankles at the first shot and now stood erect, his hands at his sides.

For a full minute Kapaloff looked at Mikhail, and then turned back to the figure at his feet. A drop of blood glistened on the toe of the shoe with which he had turned the man over. Carefully he rubbed the foot against the dead man's side until the blood was gone. Then he spoke to Mikhail, who lifted the lifeless form in his powerful arms and left the room.

Kapaloff pocketed his pistol and a courteously apologetic smile appeared on his face—as if he were a housewife who had been compelled to rebuke a maid in the presence of a guest. Phil was sick and giddy with horror, but he forced himself to accept the challenge of the smile, and said with a fair semblance of amusement: "You shouldn't have misinformed me about Serge's love for the hot knife."

Kapaloff chuckled. "The persuasion is postponed until tomorrow. I am afraid I shall have to leave you bound. Ordinarily I should simply leave Mikhail to guard you; but I am not sure that I can trust him now. Serge was his brother."

He picked up the lamp and the poniard.

"The distressing scene you have just seen should at least convince you of my earnestness." Then he left the room and the key turned in the lock.

Phil rolled over and buried his face in the bed, giving away to the sickness he had fought down in Kapaloff's presence. He lay there and sobbed, weak and miserable, and his first thought was a buoying one: the torturing had been interrupted at the last moment, almost miraculously—his luck had held!

He worked himself into a sitting position and attempted to loosen the cords around his wrists and ankles. But he only drove them deeper into the flesh, so he gave it up. He wormed his way to the floor and slowly, laboriously went over the room in the dark, hunting for something that would serve to free him; but he found nothing. The shutters were bolted and padlocked; the door was massive. He returned to the bed.

Time passed—hours he had no means of counting, and then the door opened and Mikhail came in, a tray of food in his hands. He was followed by Kapaloff who went to a window and stood with his back to it while Mikhail set the tray on the table and untied Phil.

Kapaloff gestured toward the table. "I am sorry I cannot offer you greater hospitality, but my household is disorganized. I trust you will find my humble best not too uninviting."

Phil drew a chair to the table and ate. His appetite was poor, but he forced himself to eat with every appearance of enjoyment. When the food was disposed of he lighted one of the cigarettes on the tray and smiled his thanks.

"Unless you have reconsidered," the Russian said, "I regret that you will have to sleep tied. I am sorry, but I find myself in a position where I must not let my regard for you and my sense of what is due a guest outweigh the necessity of protecting my interests."

Phil shrugged. The food had heartened him, and he was too young not to meet the challenge of his captor's manner.

"I'm tough. Mind if I stretch my legs first?"

"Not at all! I want you to be as comfortable as may be. Walk about the room and smoke. You will sleep the better for it."

Phil left the table and slowly paced up and down the room, turning over in his mind the latest development in this game. Kapaloff had entered the room behind Mikhail, had kept his right hand in his jacket pocket, and had not allowed his servant to get out of the range of his vision for an instant. If Kapaloff couldn't trust Mikhail, perhaps Phil could. The man was standing across the room from Kapaloff. His face showed nothing.

Kapaloff was asking: "You are still obdurate then, and will not make terms?"

"I'm willing to make terms—but not to accept the ones you have made."

Passing the table, Phil's glance fell on the knife with which he had cut his meat. It was silver and of little value as a weapon, but it would serve to cut the cords with which he had been bound. He reached the wall and turned. The cigarette between his lips was but a stub now. He went to the table and selected a fresh cigarette.

Reaching for a match, he placed his body between Kapaloff and the tray. Mikhail, on the other side of the room, could see every movement of Phil's hands. Fumbling with the matches, he picked up the knife with his left hand and slid it up his sleeve. Mikhail's face was expressionless.

Phil turned with the lighted cigarette in his mouth and resumed his pacing, thrusting his hands in his trouser pockets and allowing the knife to slide down into one of them. He reached the end of the room and started to turn. His elbows were seized, and he looked over his shoulder into Mikhail's stolid face.

Mikhail drew the knife from the pocket, returned it to the tray, and went back to his post by the wall.

Kapaloff spoke approvingly to Mikhail in Russian, and then said to Phil, "I did not see you get it. But, behold, you cannot put faith even in the disloyalty of my servitors!"

Phil felt tired and spent—he had counted on the scarred man's help. He went to the bed and Mikhail bound him. Then the lights were turned off and he was left alone.

The sound of a key being turned slowly, cautiously, in the door awakened Phil from the fitful sleep into which he had fallen. The noise stopped. He could see nothing. Something touched the sole of one bare foot and he jumped convulsively, shaking the bed.

"Sh-h-h!"

A cool soft hand touched his cheek, and he whispered, "Romaine?"

"Yes. Be still while I cut the cords."

Her hands passed down his arms, and his hands were freed. A little more fumbling in the dark and his feet were loose. He sat up suddenly and their faces bumped in the dark, and quite without premeditation he kissed her. For an instant she clung to him. Then she retreated a few inches, and said, "But first we must hurry."

"Sure," he agreed. "What do we do next?"

"Go downstairs to the front of the house and wait until we hear the dogs in the rear. Mikhail will call them back there under some pretext and hold them until we get out of the yard."

She pressed a heavy revolver into Phil's hand.

"But aren't the dogs kept locked up?"

"No."

"They were last night," Phil insisted, "or I never would have made it."

"Oh, yes! Uncle Boris expected you, and kept them in the garage until after you arrived."

"Oh." So he had done what was expected of him! "Well, if Mikhail's with us, why not slip down and grab your uncle and wind this thing up?"

"No! Mikhail wouldn't help us do that. Even when his brother was killed before his eyes he would do nothing! For generations his people have been serfs, slaves, of uncle's—and he hasn't the courage to defy him. If he's to help at all it must be secretly. If it comes to a point where he must choose, he will be with uncle."

"All right, let's go." His bare feet touched the floor and he laughed. "I haven't seen my shoes since I came through the window. I'm going to have a lot of fun running around on my naked tootsies!"

She took his hand and led him to the door. They listened but heard nothing. They crept out into the hall and toward the stairs. An electric light over the stairs gave a dim glow. They halted while Phil mounted the balustrade and unscrewed the bulb, shrouding the steps in darkness. At the foot of the flight they halted again, and Phil darkened the light there. Then she guided him toward the front door.

Somewhere in the night behind them a door opened. A noise of something slid across the floor. Then they heard Kapaloff's mellow tones:

"Children, you had best return to your rooms. There really is nothing else to do. If you move toward the door, you will show up in the moonlight that is shining through there. On the other hand, I have thoughtfully pushed a chair a little way down the hall from where I am, so that if even you could creep silently upon me you must inevitably collide with the chair and give me an inkling of where to send my bullets. So there is really nothing else for you to do but return to your rooms."

Huddled against the wall, Phil and Romaine said nothing, but in the hearts of each a desperate hope was born. Kapaloff chuckled as he killed their hopes.

"You need expect nothing from Mikhail. Your escape meant nothing to him, but he trusted you to exact the vengeance that he is too much for the serf to take himself. So he supplied you with a weapon, I suppose, and sent you down into the hall. Then he pretended to hear a noise—thinking that I would rush out here to fall before your bullets. Happily, I know something of the peasant mind. So when he started and pretended to hear something that my keener ears missed, I knocked him down with my pistol and came out here knowing just what to expect. Now I must insist that you return to your rooms."

Phil pressed the girl down until she lay flat on the floor, close to the wall. He stretched out in front of her, his eyes trying to dissolve the darkness. Kapaloff was lying on the floor somewhere ahead—but which wall was he clinging to? In a room something of his position could have been learned from his voice, but in this narrow passage all sense of direction was lost. The sounds simply came out of the night.

The Russian's cultured voice reached them again. "You know, we are on the verge of making ourselves ridiculous. This reclining in the dark would be well enough except that I fancy we are both exceptionally patient beings. Hence, it is likely to be prolonged to an absurd length."

With the hand that was not occupied with the revolver Phil felt in his pockets. In a vest pocket he found several coins. He tossed one of them down the hall; it hit a wall and fell to the floor.

Kapaloff laughed. "I was thinking of doing that, too; but it isn't easy to imitate the sound of a person in motion."

Phil cursed under his breath. "There must be some way out of this hole!"

Toward the front the hall was too light, as Kapaloff has said; and there seemed to be no other exits except by the stairs, or past the Russian. He might chance a volley—but there was the girl to consider. He never questioned that Kapaloff would shoot. Romaine crawled to his side.

"If we go upstairs," she whispered, "we are trapped."

"Can you think of anything?"

"No." And then she clutched his arm. "I believe he has gone. It feels as if no one else was here."

"What would that mean?"

"The dogs, maybe!"

He thought of the sinewy bodies and dripping jaws he had seen in the yard, and shuddered.

"You wait here," he ordered, and started crawling silently toward the rear of the hall.

After it seemed that he must have gone a hundred feet his hand touched the chair of which Kapaloff had spoken. He moved it aside carefully, and went on. His fingers touched a door-frame—the end of the hall.

He whispered to the girl, "He's gone," and she joined him.

"Shall we make a break for it?" he asked.

"Yes. Better try the back."

Three steps they took into the darkness, and then the lights clicked on and Phil found himself helpless, his arms pinned in Mikhail's powerful embrace. Kapaloff plucked the revolver from Phil's hand and smiled into his face.

"The variable Mikhail—whom you see allied with me again—has a tough head, and I feared that my blow would not quiet him for long. You can imagine in what an unenviable position I found myself out in the hall—with you ahead and my erratic compatriot behind. When I could stand it no longer I came back and resuscitated him, enlisting him on my side again."

Mikhail released Phil and stepped back. Kapaloff went on, with a gay mockery of plaintiveness:

"You will readily understand, Mr. Truax, that I cannot go on this way. A few more days of this and I shall be a wreck. I am a simple soul and cannot bear this distraction. You have seen Romaine. Do you accept my terms?"

Phil shook off the feeling of disgust with himself for having been so easily recaptured and decided to play the same game he had played before: bluff until the actual pain came. He smiled and shook his head. "I'm afraid we'll never agree."

Kapaloff sighed. "I shall attend to the rites myself this time; so do not expect an outburst of tenderness to halt them. Though my heart bleeds for you my hands will be steady."

Then the girl spoke. Her voice was tense, vibrant. Both men turned toward her. She was speaking to Mikhail, in Russian. Her voice gradually sank lower and lower until it was but a murmur, and took on an urgent, pleading tone.

Mikhail's lips were pressing together with increasing tension, and his carriage became rigid. His eyes fixed on a spot on the opposite wall.

Phil shot a puzzled look at Kapaloff and saw that he was watching his niece and servant with dancing eyes.

The girl's voice crooned on and moisture came out on Mikhail's face. His mouth was a thin, straight line now, and the skin over the knuckles of his clenched hands seemed about to split from strain. Still Romaine talked and, as she mentioned Serge's name, suddenly it came to Phil what was happening.

She was making an open appeal to Mikhail, reminding him of his brother's death, goading him into desperation!

The man's eyes were distended and the scar across his nose was a vivid gash—it might have been made yesterday. The muscles of his forehead, jaws, and neck stood out like welts; his breath hissed through quivering nostrils.

Still the girl's voice went on.

Phil looked at Kapaloff again. A sardonic smile of amused expectancy was on his face. He spoke softly, mockingly, a few words, but neither the girl nor Mikhail heeded him. Her voice droned on—a monotonous chant.

Mikhail's great fists opened and drops of blood ran down his fingers from where his nails had bitten into the palms. Slowly, he turned and met his master's eyes. For a second the eyes held, but Mikhail's heritage of servility was too strong within him. His eyes dropped and he shifted uneasily from one foot to the other.

The girl gave him no rest. The syllables came from her lips in a torrent, and her voice went abruptly high and sharp. Despite his unfamiliarity with the language, Phil felt his pulse drumming under the beat of her tone.

Mikhail's shoulders swayed slowly and a white froth appeared in the corners of his mouth. Then his face lost every human quality. A metallic snarl rasped from deep in his chest. Without turning, without looking, he sprang upon the man who had killed his brother.

There was no interval the eye could discern. He was standing, swaying, looking at the floor with bulging, bloodshot eyes. Then he was upon Kapaloff and they were rolling on the floor. There was no appreciable interim.

Kapaloff discharged his pistol once, but Phil could not see where the bullet hit. Over and over they rolled—Mikhail a brute gone mad, blindly fumbling for a grip on his enemy's throat; Kapaloff fighting with every trick in his cool head, and as little disturbed as if it were a game. His eyes met Phil's over Mikhail's shoulder, and he made a grimace of distaste.

Then Kapaloff twisted free, whirled to his feet, dashed a foot into the face of his rising assailant, and vanished into the dark of the hall. The kick carried Mikhail over backward, but he was up immediately, bellowing and plunging after Kapaloff.

Phil picked up the weapon Kapaloff had dropped—the revolver he had taken from Phil—and turned to the girl. Her hands were over her face and she was trembling violently. He shook her.

"Where's the phone?"

She tried twice, and finally spoke. "In the next room."

He patted her cheek. "You phone the police and wait for me here."

She clung to him for a moment, then pulled herself together, and went into the next room.

Phil moved to the hall door and listened. A scuffling sound and Kapaloff's mocking chuckle came from somewhere on the stairs. A shot thundered. Mikhail bellowed. Phil felt his way to the foot of the stairs and started up.

From above came the noise of a struggle, and Mikhail's rasping breath. Two shots. A body fell, sliding down the steps. Phil had gained the second floor and was climbing toward the third. The sliding body came toward him. He recognized it as Mikhail by the gibbering snarls it emitted. Kapaloff's laugh came from the head of the stairs.

As he braced his legs to halt Mikhail's descent, Phil raised his revolver and fired into the darkness above. Streaks of orange flame darted down at him; a bullet burned his cheek; others hit around him. Then the man at his feet was dragging him down with grim fingers that felt for his throat. He screamed into Mikhail's ear, trying to bring comprehension to the man that his enemy was above, that he was attacking an ally. But the crushing fingers felt their way higher and higher up Phil's chest, closed about his throat.

With a desperate summoning of his failing strength Phil drove his pistol into the face he could not see in the dark, and wrenched himself away. The fingers slipped, clutched at him, missed, and Phil was stumbling up the steps ahead of something that had been a man, but was now a rabid thing clambering through the night, with death in its heart and no understanding of the difference between friend and enemy.

Phil reached the top of the stairs and, not knowing it in the dark, reached for the next step, stumbled, and fell forward in the hall. As he fell Kapaloff's pistol spat, bringing down a shower of plaster. At the head of the stairs Mikhail was snarling. Phil rolled, jerking himself to one side, and pressed against the wainscoting, just in time to let the madman charge past.

Two more shots rang out.

Then a bestial voice rose in a bellow of insane triumph, a scuffle, a groan so faint that it might have been a sigh, heavy bodies falling . . . silence.

Phil got to his feet and advanced warily up the hall. His legs touched a body. Something liquid, warm and sticky, was under his bare feet.

He stumbled on and opened the first door he reached. He found the light button and pressed it. Then he turned and looked down the hall in the light that came through the open doorway . . .

He closed his eyes and groped his way to the stairs, down to the room where he had left the girl.

The girl ran to him. "Your face! You are hurt!"

"Just a scratch. I had forgotten it."

She drew his head down and dabbed at his torn cheek with a handkerchief.

"The others?" she asked.

"Dead. Did you get the police?"

She said, "Yes," and then could no longer withstand the weakness that tugged at her. She dropped into his arms, sobbing. He carried her to a couch and knelt beside her, stroking her hands and soothing her.

When she had mastered her weakness sufficiently to sit up, he asked her, more to take her mind from the gruesome termination of the affair than because his curiosity was so pressing, "Now, what's this all about?"

As she talked she gradually regained her composure, and the dread that the night's events had stirred within her subsided. Her voice grew steadier, her words more coherent, and some measure of color returned to her cheeks.

Her father had been a Russian nobleman, her mother an American. Her mother had died when Romaine was still a child. Later the little girl had been sent to a convent in the United States, in accordance with her mother's desire.

When the war broke out in Europe she had returned to Russia, despite her father's orders, with the childish thought that she would be near him. She had seen him twice before his death. He was reported "killed in action" shortly before the revolution. His brother Boris had been appointed her guardian and administrator of the estate.

Then the revolution came. Her uncle had foreseen the uprising and had converted much of the girl's wealth—he had no personal means—into money, which he had deposited in English and French banks. When they were forced to leave their native land they had considerable wealth at their disposal. For the next few years they had moved from place to place.

Her uncle had seemed filled with a strange uneasiness, and would seldom stay long in one city or country. He had taken the name of

Kapaloff and had persuaded the girl to do likewise, though he had given no reason for the change. Finally they came to the United States, lived in various cities, and then came to Burlingame.

Since their departure from Russia her uncle had been withdrawing more and more from society, and frowning upon Romaine's desire for friends. In the United States she had made no new acquaintances. He had selected the most isolated house he could find in Burlingame and had had the windows fitted with heavy shutters, and massive doors and bolts installed.

She had wondered at the change in him but had never questioned him. His manner toward her was, as always, affectionate, protecting, and generous. Except in the matter of making new acquaintances—and he was not crudely insistent there—he allowed her to indulge every whim.

Then, late the preceding Monday night, she had found the letter that was in the bag. She had found it on the library floor, had picked it up carelessly to lay it on the table, from which she supposed it had blown. Her eyes had fallen upon the word *murder,* in Russian, heavily underscored.

She read the next few words, and then feverishly read the letter from beginning to end. It had been written to her uncle by someone who apparently had been very intimate with him in Russia, and boldly threatened that unless Boris paid the money he had promised, the truth about his brother's *murder* would be published.

She could not miss the import of the letter. It could mean but one thing: that Boris, whose own means had been dissipated, had had his brother killed so that he might gain control of the estate until the child became of age.

Dazed and bewildered, she went to her room, carrying the letter with her, and threw herself across the bed. But she had something to do. She knew of only one person to whom she could turn—a prominent Los Angeles attorney, the father of one of her schoolmates.

She took what money she had, left the house, got in her roadster, and started for the city, intending to take the first train to

Los Angeles. But she had wasted too much time. Her uncle had missed the letter and, fearing the worst, had gone to her room. Not finding her there, he had come downstairs just as she drove away. He had sent Mikhail and Serge in another car to bring her back. They had done so, but the bag had been lost in the scuffle on Washington Street.

She had been imprisoned in her room until the afternoon, when she was taken to call on Phil. Her uncle had coached her carefully and she feared him too much to risk open defiance; but she had mastered her fright sufficiently to drop her purse and signal Phil. Then she had been brought back to the house and locked in. She had made one attempt to escape but had been caught at the window.

Phil tried to keep her mind on her story but he missed great stretches of it, watching her face, which, with youthful resilience, was regaining its bloom. The shadows that lingered under the eyes enhanced their beauty.

When she had finished they were silent for a moment. Phil wondered how much of the story he had missed. He cleared his throat and said, "You'll probably have to stay in Burlingame for a day or two until the police get through with their investigating. But if you'll give me that fellow's address—the Los Angeles lawyer—I'll wire him to come up and take you back with him when it's all over."

She looked puzzled. "But everything is all right now. I won't have to bother him."

"You'll need him. There'll be lots of trouble straightening out your affairs and your uncle's; and you'll have to have somebody to take care of you."

"But you are—" She stopped and the blood flooded her face.

Phil shook his head emphatically. "Listen! I would—" He stopped, cleared his throat, and tried again. "We are going to do this different. You are going to have this lawyer made your legal guardian. If you don't, the courts will probably appoint some old bum who happens to be a friend of the judge's. Then I'm going to convince him that I'm—that I'm not too tough an egg. And then well see."

A strange speech for one whose creed was: When your luck runs good, force it!

The girl frowned. "But—"

"Now don't argue! I haven't got what you might call a spotless record. Nothing so terrible maybe, but plenty that's bad enough. And another thing: you've got money, and I—well, when the cards run right I have enough to eat regular; then they run wrong . . . Anyway, we'll see. I'll do my talking to this lawyer fellow after he's made your guardian."

The doorbell forestalled the girl's answer. Phil went to the door, where four uniformed policemen stood, using their nightsticks to keep the hounds at bay. Phil led them back to the room where the girl was waiting and told his story briefly.

The grizzled sergeant in charge stared with round eyes from the girl to the youth with bloodstained bare feet, but he made no comment. Leaving one man with Phil and Romaine, he led the others upstairs.

Fifteen minutes later he returned.

"I thought you said the dead men were in the hall?"

"That's right," Phil said.

The sergeant shook his head.

"They're both dead, all right, and one of 'em is in the hall with half a dozen bullets in him. But we found the other one in one of the rooms—all mangled up—leaning over a sort of desk, with this under his arm."

He held out a sheet of notepaper to Phil. In a small, firm, regular handwriting, but thickly besmeared with blood, was written:

My dear Romaine,

Leaving you, I want to extend to both you and your new-found champion my heartiest wish that joy and happiness attend you.

My only regret is that so little of your heritage remains—but I was always careless with money! I advise you to cling to Mr. Truax—never have

I seen a more promising young man. And he has at least three hundred and fifty dollars!

There is much that I would write, but my strength is going and I fear that my pen will waver. And I who have never shown a sign of weakness in my life am vain enough to desire that I leave this gentle world with that record intact.

Affectionately,

Uncle Boris

BODIES PILED UP

THE MONTGOMERY HOTEL'S regular detective had taken his last week's rake-off from the hotel bootlegger in merchandise instead of cash, had drunk it down, had fallen asleep in the lobby, and had been fired. I happened to be the only idle operative in the Continental Detective Agency's San Francisco branch at the time, and thus it came about that I had three days of hotel-coppering while a man was being found to take the job permanently.

The Montgomery is a quiet hotel of the better sort, and so I had a very restful time of it—until the third and last day. Then things changed.

I came down into the lobby that afternoon to find Stacey, the assistant manager, hunting for me.

"One of the maids just phoned that there's something wrong up in 906," he said.

We went up to that room together. The door was open. In the center of the floor stood a maid, staring goggle-eyed at the closed door of the clothespress. From under it, extending perhaps a foot across the floor toward us, was a snake-shaped ribbon of blood.

I stepped past the maid and tried the door. It was unlocked. I opened it. Slowly, rigidly, a man pitched out into my arms—pitched out backward—and there was a six-inch slit down the back of his coat, and the coat was wet and sticky.

That wasn't altogether a surprise: the blood on the floor had prepared me for something of the sort. But when another followed him—facing me, this one, with a dark, distorted face—I dropped the one I had caught and jumped back.

And as I jumped a third man came tumbling out after the others.

From behind me came a scream and a thud as the maid fainted. I wasn't feeling any too steady myself. I'm no sensitive plant, and I've looked at a lot of unlovely sights in my time, but for weeks afterward I could see those three dead men coming out of that clothespress to pile up at my feet: coming out slowly—almost deliberately—in a ghastly game of "'follow your leader."

Seeing them, you couldn't doubt that they were really dead. Every detail of their falling, every detail of the heap in which they now lay, had a horrible certainty of lifelessness in it.

I turned to Stacey, who, deathly white himself, was keeping on his feet only by clinging to the foot of the brass bed.

"Get the woman out! Get doctors—police!"

I pulled the three dead bodies apart, laying them out in a grim row, faces up. Then I made a hasty examination of the room.

A soft hat, which fitted one of the dead men, lay in the center of the unruffled bed. The room key was in the door, on the inside. There was no blood in the room except what had leaked out of the clothespress, and the room showed no signs of having been the scene of a struggle.

The door to the bathroom was open. In the bottom of the bathtub was a shattered gin bottle, which, from the strength of the odor and the dampness of the tub, had been nearly full when broken. In one corner of the bathroom I found a small whisky glass and another under the tub. Both were dry, clean, and odorless.

The inside of the clothespress door was stained with blood from the height of my shoulder to the floor, and two hats lay in the puddle of blood on the closet floor. Each of the hats fitted one of the dead men.

That was all. Three dead men, a broken gin bottle, blood.

Stacey returned presently with a doctor, and while the doctor was examining the dead men, the police detectives arrived.

The doctor's work was soon done.

"This man," he said, pointing to one of them, "was struck on the back of the head with a small blunt instrument, and then strangled. This one"—pointing to another—"was simply strangled. And the third was stabbed in the back with a blade perhaps five inches long. They have been dead for about two hours—since noon or a little after."

The assistant manager identified two of the bodies. The man who had been stabbed—the first to fall out of the clothespress—had arrived at the hotel three days before, registering as Tudor Ingraham of Washington, D.C., and had occupied room 915, three doors away.

The last man to fall out—the one who had been simply choked—was the occupant of this room. His name was Vincent Develyn. He was an insurance broker and had made the hotel his home since his wife's death, some four years before.

The third man had been seen in Develyn's company frequently, and one of the clerks remembered that they had come into the hotel together at about five minutes after twelve this day. Cards and letters in his pockets told us that he was Homer Ansley, a member of the law firm of Lankershim and Ansley, whose offices were in the Miles Building—next door to Develyn's office.

Develyn's pockets held between $150 and $200; Ansley's wallet contained more than $100; Ingraham's pockets yielded nearly $300, and in a money belt around his waist we found $2,200 and two medium-sized unset diamonds. All three had watches—Develyn's was a valuable one—in their pockets, and Ingraham wore two rings, both of which were expensive ones. Ingraham's room key was in his pocket.

Beyond this money—whose presence would seem to indicate that robbery hadn't been the motive behind the three killings—we found nothing on any of the persons to throw the slightest light on the crime. Nor did the most thorough examination of both Ingraham's and Develyn's rooms teach us anything.

In Ingraham's room we found a dozen or more packs of carefully marked cards, some crooked dice, and an immense amount of
data on race-horses. Also we found that he had a wife who lived on
East Delavan Avenue in Buffalo, and a brother on Crutcher Street
in Dallas; as well as a list of names and addresses that we carried
off to investigate later. But nothing in either room pointed, even
indirectly, at murder.

Phels, the Police Department Bertillon man, found a number of
fingerprints in Develyn's room, but we couldn't tell whether they
would be of any value or not until he had worked them up. Though
Develyn and Ansley had apparently been strangled by hands, Phels
was unable to get prints from either their necks or their collars.

The maid who had discovered the blood said that she had
straightened up Develyn's room between ten and eleven that morning, but had not put fresh towels in the bathroom. It was for this
purpose that she had gone to the room in the afternoon. She had
gone there earlier—between 10:20 and 10:45—for that purpose,
but Ingraham had not then left it.

The elevator man who had carried Ansley and Develyn up from
the lobby at a few minutes after twelve remembered that they had
been laughingly discussing their golf scores of the previous day
during the ride. No one had seen anything suspicious in the hotel around the time at which the doctor had placed the murders.
But that was to be expected.

The murderer could have left the room, closing the door
behind him, and walked away secure in the knowledge that at
noon a man in the corridors of the Montgomery would attract
little attention. If he was staying at the hotel he would simply
have gone to his room; if not, he piled have either walked all
the way down to the street, or down a floor or two and then
caught an elevator.

None of the hotel employees had ever seen Ingraham and Develyn together. There was nothing to show that they had even the
slightest acquaintance. Ingraham habitually stayed in his room un-

til noon, and did not return to it until late at night. Nothing was known of his affairs.

At the Miles Building we—that is, Marty O'Hara and George Dean of the Police Department Homicide Detail, and I—questioned Ansley's partner and Develyn's employees. Both Develyn and Ansley, it seemed, were ordinary men who led ordinary lives: lives that held neither dark spots nor queer kinks. Ansley was married and had two children; he lived on Lake Street. Both men had a sprinkling of relatives and friends scattered here and there through the country; and, so far as we could learn, their affairs were in perfect order.

They had left their offices this day to go to luncheon together, intending to visit Develyn's room first for a drink apiece from a bottle of gin someone coming from Australia had smuggled in to him.

"Well," O'Hara said, when we were on the street again, "this much is clear. If they went up to Develyn's room for a drink, it's a cinch that they were killed almost as soon as they got in the room. Those whisky glasses you found were dry and clean. Whoever turned the trick must have been waiting for them. I wonder about this fellow Ingraham."

"I'm wondering, too," I said. "Figuring it out from the positions I found them in when I opened the closet door, Ingraham sizes up as the key to the whole thing. Develyn was back against the wall, with Ansley in front of him, both facing the door. Ingraham was facing them, with his back to the door. The clothespress was just large enough for them to be packed in it—too small for them to slip down while the door was closed.

"Then there was no blood in the room except what had come from the clothespress. Ingraham, with that gaping slit in his back, couldn't have been stabbed until he was inside the closet, or he'd have bled elsewhere. He was standing close to the other men when he was knifed, and whoever knifed him closed the door quickly afterward.

"Now, why should he have been standing in such a position? Do you dope it out that he and another killed the two friends, and that while he was stowing their bodies in the closet his accomplice finished him off?"

"Maybe," Dean said.

And that "maybe" was still as far as we had gone three days later.

We had sent and received bales of telegrams, having relatives and acquaintances of the dead men interviewed; and we had found nothing that seemed to have any bearing upon their deaths. Nor had we found the slightest connecting link between Ingraham and the other two. We had traced those other two back step by step almost to their cradles. We had accounted for every minute of their time since Ingraham had arrived in San Francisco—thoroughly enough to convince us that neither of them had met Ingraham.

Ingraham, we had learned, was a bookmaker and all around crooked gambler. His wife and he had separated, but were on good terms. Some fifteen years before, he had been convicted of "assault with intent to kill" in Newark, N.J., and had served two years in the state prison. But the man he had assaulted had died of pneumonia in Omaha in 1914.

Ingraham had come to San Francisco for the purpose of opening a gambling club, and all our investigations had tended to show that his activities while in the city had been toward that end alone.

The fingerprints Phels had secured had all turned out to belong to Stacey, the maid, the police detectives, or myself. In short, we had found nothing!

So much for our attempts to learn the motive behind the three murders.

We now dropped that angle and settled down to the detail-studying, patience-taxing grind of picking up the murderer's trail. From any crime to its author there is a trail. It may be—as in this case—obscure; but, since matter cannot move without disturbing other matter along its path, there always is—there must be—a trail of some sort. And finding and following such trails is what a detective is paid to do.

In the case of a murder it is possible sometimes to take a short-cut to the end of the trail, by first finding the motive. A knowledge of the motive often reduces the field of possibilities; sometimes points directly to the guilty one.

So far, all we knew about the motive in the particular case we were dealing with was that it hadn't been robbery; unless something we didn't know about had been stolen—something of sufficient value to make the murderer scorn the money in his victims' pockets.

We hadn't altogether neglected the search for the murderer's trail, of course, but—being human—we had devoted most of our attention to trying to find a short-cut. Now we set out to find our man, or men, regardless of what had urged him or them to commit the crimes.

Of the people who had been registered at the hotel on the day of the killing there were nine men of whose innocence we hadn't found a reasonable amount of proof. Four of these were still at the hotel, and only one of that four interested us very strongly. That one—a big raw-boned man of forty-five or fifty, who had registered as J. J. Cooper of Anaconda, Montana—wasn't, we had definitely established, really a mining man, as he pretended to be. And our telegraphic communications with Anaconda failed to show that he was known there. Therefore we were having him shadowed—with few results.

Five men of the nine had departed since the murders; three of them leaving forwarding addresses with the mail clerk. Gilbert Jacquemart had occupied room 946 and had ordered his mail forwarded to him at a Los Angeles hotel. W. F. Salway, who had occupied room 1022, had given instructions that his mail be readdressed to a number on Clark Street in Chicago. Ross Orrett, room 609, had asked to have his mail sent to him care of General Delivery at the local post office.

Jacquemart had arrived at the hotel two days before, and had left on the afternoon of the murders. Salway had arrived the day before the murders and had left the day after them. Orrett had arrived the day of the murders and had left the following day.

Sending telegrams to have the first two found and investigated, I went after Orrett myself. A musical comedy named *What For?* was being widely advertised just then with gaily printed plum-colored handbills. I got one of them and, at a stationery store, an envelope to match, and mailed it to Orrett at the Montgomery Hotel. There are concerns that make a practice of securing the names of arrivals at the principal hotels and mailing them advertisements. I trusted that Orrett, knowing this, wouldn't be suspicious when my gaudy envelope, forwarded from the hotel, reached him through the General Delivery window.

Dick Foley—the Agency's shadow specialist—planted himself in the post office, to loiter around with an eye on the 'O' window until he saw my plum-colored enveloped passed out, and then to shadow the receiver.

I spent the next day trying to solve the mysterious J. J. Cooper's game, but he was still a puzzle when I knocked off that night.

At a little before five the following morning Dick Foley dropped into my room on his way home to wake me up and tell me what he had done.

"This Orrett baby is our meat!" he said. "Picked him up when he got his mail yesterday afternoon. Got another letter besides yours. Got an apartment on Van Ness Avenue. Took it the day after the killing, under the name of B. T. Quinn. Packing a gun under his left arm-- there's that sort of a bulge there. Just went home to bed. Been visiting all the dives in North Beach. Who do you think he's hunting for?"

"Who?"

"Guy Cudner."

That was news! This Guy Cudner, alias "The Darkman," was the most dangerous bird on the Coast, if not in the country. He had only been nailed once, but if he had been convicted of all the crimes that everybody knew he had committed he'd have needed half a dozen lives to crowd his sentences into, besides another half-dozen to carry to the gallows. However, he had de-cidedly the right sort of backing—enough to buy him everything he needed—in the way of witnesses, alibis, even juries and an occasional judge.

I don't know what went wrong with his support that one time he was convicted up North and sent over for a one-to-fourteen-year hitch; but it adjusted itself promptly, for the ink was hard-ly dry on the press notices of his conviction before he was loose again on parole.

"Is Cudner in town?"

"Don't know," Dick said, "but this Orrett, or Quinn, or whatever his name is, is surely hunting for him. In Rick's place, at "Wop" Healey's, and at Pigatti's. "Porky" Grout tipped me off. Says Or-rett doesn't know Cudner by sight, but is trying to find him. Porky didn't know what he wants with him."

This Porky Grout was a dirty little rat who would sell out his family—if he ever had one—for the price of a flop. But with these lads who play both sides of the game it's always a question of which side they're playing when you think they're playing yours.

"Think Porky was coming clean?" I asked.

"Chances are—but you can't gamble on him."

"Is Orrett acquainted here?"

"Doesn't seem to be. Knows where he wants to go but has to ask how to get there. Hasn't spoken to anybody that seemed to know him."

"What's he like?"

"Not the kind of egg* you'd want to tangle with offhand, if you ask me. He and Cudner would make a good pair. They don't look alike. This egg is tall and slim, but he's built right—those fast, smooth muscles. Face is sharp without being thin, if you get me. I mean all the lines in it are straight. No curves. Chin, nose, mouth, eyes—all straight, sharp lines and angles. Looks like the

---

* person

198

kind of egg we know Cudner is. Make a good pair. Dresses well and doesn't look like a rowdy—but harder than hell! A big-game hunter! Our meat, I bet you!"

"It doesn't look bad," I agreed. "He came to the hotel the morning of the day the men were killed, and checked out the next morning. He packs a rod, and changed his name after he left. And now he's paired off with The Darkman. It doesn't look bad at all!"

"I'm telling you," Dick said, "this fellow looks like three killings wouldn't disturb his rest any. I wonder where Cudner fits in."

"I can't guess. But, if he and Orrett haven't connected yet, then Cudner, wasn't in on the murders; but he may give us the answer."

Then I jumped out of bed. "I'm going to gamble on Porky's dope being on the level! How would you describe Cudner?"

"You know him better than I do."

"Yes, but how would you describe him to me if I didn't know him?"

"A little fat guy with a red forked scar on his left cheek. What's the idea?"

"It's a good one," I admitted. "That scar makes all the difference in the world. If he didn't have it and you were to describe him you'd go into all the details of his appearance. But he has it, so you simply say, 'A little fat guy with a red forked scar on his left cheek.' It's a ten to one that that's just how he has been described to Orrett. I don't look like Cudner, but I'm his size and build, and with a scar on my face Orrett will fall for me."

"What then?"

"There's no telling; but I ought to be able to learn a lot if I can get Orrett talking to me as Cudner. It's worth a try anyway."

"You can't get away with it—not in San Francisco. Cudner is too well-known."

"What difference does that make, Dick? Orrett is the only one I want to fool. If he takes me for Cudner, well and good. If he doesn't, still well and good. I won't force myself on him."

"How are you going to fake the scar?"

"Easy! We have pictures of Cudner, showing the scar, in the criminal gallery. I'll get some collodion—it's sold in drug stores under several trade names for putting on cuts and scratches—color it, and imitate Cudner's scar on my cheek. It dries with a shiny surface and, put on thick, will stand out enough to look like an old scar."

It was a little after eleven the following night when Dick telephoned me that Orrett was in Pigatti's place, on Pacific Street, and apparently settled there for some little while. My scar already painted on, I jumped into a taxi and within a few minutes was talking to Dick, around the corner from Pigatti's.

"He's sitting at the last table back on the left side. And he was alone when I came out. You can't miss him. He's the only egg in the joint with a clean collar."

"You better stick outside—half a block or so away—with the taxi," I told Dick. "Maybe brother Orrett and I will leave together and I'd just as leave have you standing by in case things break wrong."

Pigatti's place is a long, narrow, low-ceilinged cellar, always dim with smoke. Down the middle runs a narrow strip of bare floor for dancing. The rest of the floor is covered with closely packed tables, whose cloths are always soiled.

Most of the tables were occupied when I came in, and half a dozen couples were dancing. Few of the faces to be seen were strangers to the morning "line-up" at police headquarters.

Peering through the smoke, I saw Orrett at once, seated alone in a far corner, looking at the dancers with the set blank face of one who masks an all-seeing watchfulness. I walked down the other side of the room and crossed the strip of dance-floor directly under a light, so that the scar might be clearly visible to him. Then I selected a vacant table not far from his, and sat down facing him.

Ten minutes passed while he pretended an interest in the dancers and I affected a thoughtful stare at the dirty cloth on my table; but neither of us missed so much as a flicker of the other's lids.

His eyes—gray eyes that were pale without being shallow, with black needle-point pupils—met mine after a while in a cold, steady, inscrutable stare; and, very slowly, he got to his feet. One hand—his right—in a side pocket of his dark coat, he walked straight across to my table and sat down.

"Cudner?"

"Looking for me, I hear," I replied, trying to match the icy smoothness of his voice, as I was matching the steadiness of his gaze.

He had sat down with his left side turned slightly toward me, which put his right arm in not too cramped a position for straight shooting from the pocket that still held his hand.

"You were looking for me, too."

I didn't know what the correct answer to that would be, so I just grinned. But the grin didn't come from my heart. I had, I realized, made a mistake—one that might cost me something before we were done. This bird wasn't hunting for Cudner as a friend, as I had carelessly assumed, but was on the war path.

I saw those three dead men falling out of the closet in room 906!

My gun was inside the waist-band of my trousers, where I could get it quickly, but his was in his hand. So I was careful to keep my own hands motionless on the edge of the table, while I widened my grin.

His eyes were changing now, and the more I looked at them the less I liked them. The gray in them had darkened and grown duller, and the pupils were larger, and white crescents were showing beneath the gray. Twice before I had looked into eyes such as these—and I hadn't forgotten what they meant—the eyes of the congenital killer!

"Suppose you speak your piece," I suggested after a while.

But he wasn't to be beguiled into conversation. He shook his head a mere fraction of an inch and the corners of his compressed mouth dropped down a trifle. The white crescents of eyeballs were growing broader, pushing the gray circles up under the upper lids.

It was coming! And there was no use waiting for it!

I drove a foot at his shins under the table, and at the same time pushed the table into his lap and threw myself across it.

The bullet from his gun went off to one side. Another bullet—not from his gun—thudded into the table that was upended between us.

I had him by the shoulders when the second shot from behind took him in the left arm, just below my hand. I let go then and fell away, rolling over against the wall and twisting around to face the direction from which the bullets were coming.

I twisted around just in time to see—jerking out of sight behind a corner of the passage that gave to a small dining-room—Guy Cudner's scarred face. And as it disappeared a bullet from Orrett's gun splattered the plaster from the wall where it had been.

I grinned at the thought of what must be going on in Orrett's head as he lay sprawled out on the floor confronted by two Cudners. But he took a shot at me just then and I stopped grinning. Luckily, he had to twist around to fire at me, putting his weight on his wounded arm, and the pain made him wince, spoiling his aim.

Before he had adjusted himself more comfortably I had scrambled on hands and knees to Pigatti's kitchen door—only a few feet away—and had myself safely tucked out of range around an angle in the wall; all but my eyes and the top of my head, which I risked so that I might see what went on.

Orrett was now ten or twelve feet from me, lying flat on the floor, facing Cudner, with a gun in his hand and another on the floor beside him.

Across the room, perhaps thirty feet away, Cudner was showing himself around his protecting corner at brief intervals to exchange shots with the man on the floor, occasionally sending one my way. We had the place to ourselves. There were four exits, and the rest of Pigatti's customers had used them all.

I had my gun out, but I was playing a waiting game. Cudner, I figured, had been tipped off to Orrett's search for him and had arrived on the scene with no mistaken idea of the other's attitude. Just what there was between them and what bearing it had on the Montgomery murders was a mystery to me, but I didn't try to solve it now.

They were firing in unison. Cudner would show around his corner, both men's weapons would spit, and he would duck out of sight again. Orrett was bleeding about the head now and one of his legs sprawled crookedly behind him. I couldn't determine whether Cudner had been hit or not.

Each had fired eight, or perhaps nine, shots when Cudner suddenly jumped out into full view, pumping the gun in his left hand as fast as its mechanism would go, the gun in his right hand hanging at his side. Orrett had changed guns, and was on his knees now, his fresh weapon keeping pace with his enemy's.

That couldn't last!

Cudner dropped his left-hand gun, and, as he raised the other, he sagged forward and went down on one knee. Orrett stopped firing abruptly and fell over on his back—spread out full-length. Cudner fired once more—wildly, into the ceiling—and pitched down on his face.

I sprang to Orrett's side and kicked both of his guns away. He was lying still but his eyes were open.

"Are you Cudner, or was he?"

"He."

"Good!" he said, and closed his eyes.

I crossed to where Cudner lay and turned him over on his back. His chest was literally shot to pieces.

His thick lips worked, and I put my ear down to them. "I get him?"

"Yes," I lied, "he's already cold."

His dying face twisted into a grin.

"Sorry . . . three in hotel . . . ," he gasped hoarsely. "Mistake . . . wrong room . . . got one . . . had to . . . other two . . . protect myself . . . I . . ." He shuddered and died.

A week later the hospital people let me talk to Orrett. I told him what Cudner had said before he died.

"That's the way I doped it out," Orrett said from out of the depths of the bandages in which he was swathed. "That's why I moved and changed my name the next day.

"I suppose you've got it nearly figured out by now," he said after a while.

"No," I confessed, "I haven't. I've an idea what it was all about but I could stand having a few details cleared up."

"I'm sorry I can't clear them up for you, but I've got to cover myself up. I'll tell you a story, though, and it may help you. Once upon a time there was a high-class crook—what the newspapers call a master-mind. Came a day when he found he had accumulated enough money to give up the game and settle down as an honest man.

"But he had two lieutenants—one in New York and one in San Francisco—and they were the only men in the world who knew he was a crook. And, besides that, he was afraid of both of them. So he thought he'd rest easier if they were out of the way. And it happened that neither of these lieutenants had ever seen the other.

"So this master-mind convinced each of them that the other was double-crossing him and would have to be bumped off for the safety of all concerned. And both of them fell for it. The New Yorker went to San Francisco to get the other, and the San Franciscan was told that the New Yorker would arrive on such-and-such a day and would stay at such-and-such a hotel.

"The master-mind figured that there was an even chance of both men passing out when they met—and he was nearly right at that. But he was sure that one would die, and then, even if the other missed hanging, there would only be one man left for him to dispose of later."

There weren't as many details in the story as I would have liked to have, but it explained a lot.

"How do you figure out Cudner's getting the wrong room?" I asked.

"That was funny! Maybe it happened like this: My room was 609 and the killing was done in 906. Suppose Cudner went to the hotel on the day he knew I was due and took a quick slant at the register. He wouldn't want to be seen looking at it if he could avoid it, so he didn't turn it around, but flashed a look at it as it lay—facing the desk.

"When you read numbers of three figures upside-down you have to transpose them in your head to get them straight. Like 123. You'd get that 321, and then turn them around in your head. That's what Cudner did with mine. He was keyed up, of course, thinking of the job ahead of him, and he overlooked the fact that 609 upside-down still reads 609 just the same. So he turned it around and made it 906—Develyn's room."

"That's how I doped it," I said, "and I reckon it's about right. And then he looked at the key-rack and saw that 906 wasn't there. So he thought he might just as well get his job done right then, when he could roam the hotel corridors without attracting attention. Of course, he may have gone up to the room before Ansley and Develyn came in and waited for them, but I doubt it.

"I think it more likely that he simply happened to arrive at the hotel a few minutes after they had come in. Ansley was probably alone in the room when Cudner opened the unlocked door and came in—Develyn being in the bathroom getting the glasses.

"Ansley was about your size and age, and close enough in appearance to fit a rough description of you. Cudner went for him, and then Develyn, hearing the scuffle, dropped the bottle and glasses, rushed out, and got his.

"Cudner, being the sort he was, would figure that two murders were not worse than one, and he wouldn't want to leave any witnesses around.

"And that is probably how Ingraham got into it. He was passing on his way from his room to the elevator and perhaps heard the racket and investigated. And Cudner put a gun in his face and made him stow the two bodies in the clothespress. And then he stuck his knife in Ingraham's back and slammed the door on him. That's about the—"

An indignant nurse descended on me from behind and ordered me out of the room, accusing me of getting her patient excited.

Orrett stopped me as I turned to go.

"Keep your eye on the New York dispatches," he said, "and maybe you'll get the rest of the story. It's not over yet. Nobody has anything on me out here. That shooting in Pigatti's was self-defence so far as I'm concerned. And as soon as I'm on my feet again and can get back East there's going to be a master-mind holding a lot of lead. That's a promise!"

I believed him.

www.ingramcontent.com/pod-product-compliance
Lightning Source LLC
Chambersburg PA
CBHW021036130626
46552CB00005B/1865